"It's them!" Kidd shouted, grinning at the thought of the ransom. "Mills!"

"Wrong man," Willie muttered, as he raised his own rifle and fired. Joe must have done so, too, for a pair of bullets struck Murphy simultaneously. The first lifted him off the ground, and the second slammed him down hard.

"Murph?" Kidd called, as he scrambled behind the tent.

"He's dead!" Joe shouted, as he splashed through the creek and gained the safety of the horses. "You'll be, too, soon enough."

"Ain't you forgettin' somethin'?" Ben Calder shouted, dragging Jake along like a shield. The scrawny eleven-year-old didn't provide much cover, but Willie held his fire just the same.

The elder Calder grabbed his rifle and crept cautiously toward the creek. Dewey shot him in the throat.

"Where's the money?" Kidd screamed.

Also by G. Clifton Wisler
Published by Fawcett Gold Medal Books:

Blood Mesa

G. Clifton Wisler

FAWCETT GOLD MEDAL • NEW YORK

Remembering Todd Evans
(1973–1990)
who knew the river and the midnight sky

CHAPTER 1

West Texas was hard country—rock and sand, buffalo grass and prickly pear.

"Just the leavings, son," Willie's father had once proclaimed. "When God tired of trees and meadows and lakes, he got around to Texas."

So it often seemed, even in the gentler seasons of autumn and spring. Now it was winter, and the stark ridges and rock-strewn streams were alternately frozen gray or white, depending on whether fresh snow had happened along. Even when it hadn't there was a scent of death to the land, a hush whispered by the bare branches of oaks and willows down by the river or else carried by the scant deer doing their best to survive on what little forage remained.

"This land weeds out the weak, Willie," Bill Delamer had once declared. "Refines the breed, so to speak. Puts iron in your backbone. Yes, sir, makes you strong."

"Or buries you," Willie muttered, remembering the brother he'd helped bury along the Brazos. Big Bill himself rested in that rock-hard ground, laid low by Yank bullets at Shiloh. A hundred times Willie had cursed that barren, empty country for the hardships it had brought him, the pain and the loss. Even so, the place was home.

1

And it had drawn him back from tall mountains and roaring rivers.

Willie placed his numb fingers in his armpits and hugged himself. A shudder worked its way through him. As if that weren't enough a gust of frigid February wind hit him, sending icy darts through every inch of exposed flesh. His weathered buffalo-hide coat lacked the power to fend off the cold, and his legs wobbled.

"Why?" he called to the gray skies. Hadn't that country known enough hard times? Couldn't the wind at least ease its torments?

He slapped his hands against his sides and coughed icy clouds of steamy breath. Willie stared at the ax standing idle beside a woodpile. There would be need of logs for the fireplace, and he dared not ask one of the boys to attempt the task. They were frail enough, and young to boot. As he had never been.

"It's winter's way to steal in and carry off the little ones," he'd told Ellen.

"It's no worse here than in Kansas," she'd barked. "And they're tougher than you think."

You're their mother, Willie thought, but even you don't know. Texas is a thief, eager to rob faith and health. It only leaves you death and pain.

He stared at the river a moment, recalling better days. This was the Salt Fork of the Brazos, appropriately named, for its waters attested to the minerals absorbed on their long journey across the barrens of the Llano, bound for south Texas and the Gulf of Mexico. Willie remembered the time he'd crossed those very banks as a skinny boy of fourteen, racing to keep pace with Red Wolf. That Comanche had a knack for leaving a boy behind, or else running him into a deer thicket or a nest of pencil cactus. Not even Red Wolf was a match for the yellow-haired terror of the river bottoms that young Willie had been.

"That was another lifetime," Willie mumbled, shaking the recollection from his head. Red Wolf and his people were dead. The buffalo were gone. And Willie Delamer wore a strange name in the very land of his birth.

"Uncle Wil, you coming in to breakfast?" a young voice called from the far side of the woodpile.

"Not today," Willie replied, grinning slightly at the sight of Ellen's eldest, ten-year-old Billy. Still half a foot shy of five foot, and not eighty pounds even smothered in his buffalo-hide coat, the boy planted a hand on each hip and tried to glare. The lips too soon formed a smile, though, as Willie trotted over and rested a weary hand on the youngster's shoulder.

"Mama's going to be mad," Billy complained.

"Got to check the stock, son," Willie replied. "I'll chew a biscuit on the way."

"Seems to me you got time to eat proper," Billy grumbled. "Joe ain't even here yet. How you figure to get Mama to marry you if you never see her?"

"I never knew I was trying," Willie answered.

"Oh? Then how come you call me 'son'?"

"I call lots of boys that," Willie said, stepping away.

"Well, maybe, but you don't go looking at their mamas like you do mine. Wouldn't be such a bad bargain, after all. She's pretty, and she cooks better'n most. And you'd have us four kids thrown in to boot. It's about time you jumped right in and got it done."

"Be a mighty big jump," Willie said, laughing.

"Mama won't get any younger, you know. And you ain't so good-looking as to have lots of choices."

Willie laughed again, then nudged the boy back toward the house. Billy reached the door, then turned and offered a silent plea. The boy's clear blue eyes held so much of their mother's that Willie froze in his tracks.

"They could be yours," Ellen had said only last night. "In some ways, they are. They miss their papa, Willie. They want a man, and you're the best one I've ever known, discounting Jack."

"You married the right one," he'd answered.

"He's dead now. You're not."

"You're wrong, Ellie. I've been dead since I don't know when. Maybe it was the snows at Petersburg did me in. Maybe it was coming home to find Mama buried, my brothers changed, no place left for me to belong to."

"But we've got a new chance here!" she'd cried. "A fresh start!"

"Do we?" he'd asked. "For how long? Till winter freezes us? Till my brother Sam finds out I've come back to Texas? Till some fuzzy-cheeked kid decides to find out if Wil Fletcher's scared of him?"

She'd had no answer—not then nor now. And as Willie stared at the Brazos rolling relentlessly along, he fought to forget. Another year he would have ridden off in search of peace, but he knew better. The blizzards of '80 had been particularly daunting, and he was needed here. Moreover, a man alone in this inhospitable country didn't stand an icicle's chance in hell.

His thoughts were broken by the sound of an approaching rider. As the horseman neared, Willie identified the leathery brown face as belonging to Joe Eagle.

"See anything?" Willie called to the Cheyenne.

"No cows north," Joe answered. "Nothin's crossin' Salt Fork, either. River's up six, seven feet upstream."

Willie stared at the swollen banks of the Salt Fork and nodded his agreement. Close to a hundred longhorns had been grazing south of the house before the last storm hit. Now they were likely scattered across half of Throckmorton County. Running them back home would take time— assuming they could be found.

"There's somethin' to be said for fencin'," Joe announced as he pulled his horse closer. "Settles down the range work considerable."

"I don't mind it much," Willie declared, as he shook off the chill and mounted a waiting horse. "Gives a man purpose, riding the range."

"If it don't kill him," Joe muttered. "And for what? A

hundred steers! You fence your acreage, you'd pick up a lot o' mavericks, Major. And you wouldn't worry over them range bandits helpin' themselves to your beeves.''

"I don't worry about them now," Wil said, laughing. He pushed back a handful of sandy blond hair from his forehead and adjusted the weathered gray cavalry hat that had become a trademark of sorts. "What've I got to interest them?"

Joe shook his head and mumbled a Cheyenne curse. The two of them then turned south to continue the search for the wayward beasts.

They rode three miles before heading onto the treeless plain south and west of the river. Except for the stumps of scrub mesquite that mixed with the buffalo grass and yucca, that stretch was utterly barren. In summer it was a sweltering inferno. Now, with the cold and the endless whining of the wind . . .

"Seems haunted, even in daylight," Joe remarked.

"No, just empty," Willie muttered. Lately it seemed life itself was that way. So many of the old dreams had been buried along some rocky stretch of barren country! And now, back home where he'd taken his first steps, ridden his first pony, first hunted and laughed and loved, the landscape itself seemed to be changing.

I'm not even myself, Willie thought. Most knew him as Fletcher. Fletcher! Another alias picked up in a decade and a half of wandering. Only a few knew of Willie Delamer. And those who did remembered the wartime hero, leader of men, baffler of bluecoat cavalry, and devil raider along the Rappahannock. Only Ellen recalled the shaggy-haired boy who had haunted the Brazos bottoms and ridden bareback with the Comanches out on the Llano.

Ellen. Just thinking of her brought a surge of warmth flowing through his chest. Her delicate hands, those bright, shining eyes lighting up the darkest moments . . .

"There's some over there," Joe announced, breaking into Willie's thoughts.

"I see 'em," Willie replied, as he nudged his horse in that direction. Soon he was circling around the grazing steers and driving them northward, back toward Salt Fork Crossing. Joe Eagle had located a second batch and was likewise urging them north, when he reined in his horse and pointed southward.

At first Willie didn't note anything out of the ordinary. Then he sniffed something—smoke. Finally he spotted a thin gray curl rising from beyond a rock-studded hill three hundred yards away.

"Visitors," Joe called, drawing his Winchester rifle from its saddle scabbard. "Go easy."

"Always do," Willie said, frowning. "There's a ravine cuts that ridge, Joe. I'll take the lead. Hang back a step or two till I see what's up."

"Don't you ride in on strangers, Major," Joe advised. "Some of 'em's jittery come winter."

"Turning cautious, Joe? Most likely out-of-work cowboys, or else boys out hunting."

"Could be my dead grandma, too," Joe grumbled. "Been rustlers hereabouts. You do recall that."

"I do. But I never knew thieves to light fires or leave a clear trail," Willie said, pointing to the traces of hoof prints in the sandy soil. "Anyway, we're about to find out."

Joe shook his head, but he did as instructed. Willie urged his horse into a slow trot and headed onward.

They were ten minutes traversing the ravine. When they finally emerged on the far side of the ridge, Willie drew up short. Just ahead two figures huddled beside a meager fire. A steer's hide lay draped over a skinning rack a few feet away.

"Morning, boys," Willie called to the strangers.

The one on the right jumped to his feet and fumbled with a pistol.

"I'd leave that be," Joe Eagle said, moving past Willie and swinging his rifle to bear.

"Don't stray too far," Willie warned, as the other figure turned away from the fire.

"I suppose you got a reason for pointin' that Winchester at us," the first man, a youngish fellow with dusty brown hair, complained as he dropped his revolver. "You might keep that horse back a hair. I ain't fond o' stirrin' dust in with my breakfast."

"Wouldn't want that," Willie said, glaring at them with icy blue eyes. "Brazos beef makes good eating. Guess you brought that steer along with you."

"You know we didn't," the other one barked. "What's your play, mister? You aim to shoot us for butcherin' a range steer?"

"We've had lots of trouble this winter with bandits," Joe announced. "Runnin' off cattle, horses, livin' out here like they owned the place."

"I look to own anything?" the first man asked, opening his coat. Willie noted the young man's threadbare cotton shirt and thin frame.

"Got a name, I suppose," Willie answered.

"Warren Rucker," he said, shifting his weight. "That's my brother Polk there."

"Knew a Rucker once," Willie told them.

"Ain't any law against bein' one," Polk declared. "We done nothin' wrong."

"We crossed no fences," Warren added. "Figured this stretch was still open range."

"Cattle have brands," Willie pointed out.

"Some do, and some don't," Polk observed. "We put a rope on a pure maverick, mister, though I'll admit if I was hungrier I'd likely run down anything on four feet. Always been a sort o' law out here that a hungry man can feed himself off a range cow."

"That time's passed," Joe declared. "Been men hung for skinnin' out steers in this country."

"And who'd you be to hang us?" Warren growled.

"Fletcher," Willie explained. "Marshal of Esperanza,"

he added, opening his hide coat to reveal a shiny metal star. "Also happens I hold title to this acreage."

"Then I guess you'll do what you want," Warren said, eyeing his discarded gun. "We been all winter fightin' long odds and hard times. Guess it was bound to come to this."

"You won't find hangin' me so easy a job," Polk warned, bending over and picking up a log. "You feel ready to try, come on."

"He always this excitable?" Willie asked, sliding off his horse. "Or is it he gets this way around lawmen?"

"He's just turned seventeen," Warren explained, taking off his hat and slapping it against his knee. "Just a boy really. Still growin' his first chin whiskers. Winter's addled him some."

"I'm old enough to give you a fair test," Polk promised.

"Be short work for Joe's Winchester," Willie countered. "But I never had much stomach for hanging anybody, and especially not somebody with the look of a cowboy. Got some coffee in yon pot? I missed my breakfast this morning."

"Tastes more like gunpowder, but you're welcome to some," Warren said, producing a tin cup. "Polk, this fire could use that log. Toss her on. Your Indian friend care to partake?"

"He's uneasy around strangers," Willie explained, as he poured himself a cup of coffee. It tasted as advertised, and he winced. "Now *that's* a hanging offense, boys."

"We're low on beans, Marshal," Warren confessed.

"Low on everything," Polk added. "Been three months tryin' to get north to our uncle's place up on the Little Wichita."

"Floods," Warren muttered.

"You were south then," Willie said, forcing the coffee down. "Find range work there?"

"Summer and fall," Warren explained. "On the Austin Ranch, down in Hood County. Ole Austin had some bad luck at the poker table, and firin' us covered some o' his losses.''

"Fired us without so much as a 'good mornin' ','' Polk said bitterly. "Been that way with us ever since the war. Bad luck turnin' to worse.''

"I've known some hard times myself," Willie told them. "And Joe there, well, there's some that's known worse.''

"Worse?'' Warren asked. "Yanks kilt my pa. Fever took Ma. Been on our own since rememberin'.''

"It's good you've got an uncle to take you in," Willie said.

"Marshal, Uncle Riley's got his own troubles. Five kids, and he's taken in Uncle Jube's young ones and some others, too," Warren said, slapping his hat again. "Ain't any parade welcomin' us there. But he'll have straw in his barn, and there's fair huntin' up that way.''

"We'd hoped to bring some cash with us, but all we got's a pair o' silver dollars," Polk muttered. "And likely we owe you that for the steer we butchered.''

"No, keep it," Willie said, frowning. "Have your feed, and smoke what's left. But you get along up north. You can't expect everyone hereabouts to look at you with a friendly eye.''

"I guess not," Warren agreed. "You wouldn't know where we could come by work?''

"Just farmers here, mostly," Willie told them. "Fellow named Mills has a ranch across the river. . . .''

"Stay clear o' him," Joe advised. "He's lost beef to rustlers, and he'd hang a stranger fast.''

"You said you were the marshal," Polk said, frowning. "How is it he can hang anybody?''

"Town marshal's got little say-so out in the county," Willie explained. "And Mills isn't the kind to ask for advice.''

"We'd never get across the river anyhow," Warren pointed out. "We'll head north. Maybe the weather'll break, and the river will drop.''

"Might," Willie said, handing the young man his empty cup. "Wish you well. Watch out you don't get crosswise to trouble."

"Do our best," Warren replied. "And we'll clear out fast as we can, Marshal."

"See you do," Willie said, giving them a final stern glance. Then he climbed back atop his horse and turned the animal back toward the ravine.

"Figure they're the rustlers, Wil?" Joe asked, when they started up the ridge.

"Not too likely," Willie said, shaking his head. "I knew their pa. Was with me when we tangled with the Michigan cavalry back in Virginia."

"You didn't tell them."

"They wouldn't recognize any Wil Fletcher. Besides, that was a long time ago. I hope they get along to Riley's place fast. The whole country's up in arms over hiders and rustlers."

"Better to be a Cheyenne than one of them," Joe mused.

"World's pure gone crazy, Joe. Half-starved boys riding the range, and old renegades like us holding guns on them."

"Best to be careful," Joe advised. "Lots better'n bein' dead."

CHAPTER 2

Willie devoted the rest of the morning and most of the afternoon to driving the stray cattle back toward the river. Twice he and Joe Eagle spied the Rucker brothers. The young cowboys were busy smoking beef the first time. Later Willie spotted them riding north.

"They worry you?" Joe asked, when Willie turned to follow.

"Not much," Willie answered.

"I could trail 'em a ways. See 'em clear o' Esperanza."

"I'd rather have you keep an eye on the stock," Willie declared. "After all, I have to show my face in town every once in a while. Otherwise folks will wonder what they're paying me a marshal's wage for."

"Twenty dollars a month," Joe grumbled. "And you pass on half o' that to me. They ain't payin' anybody much."

"Well, there's some truth there," Willie agreed. "I'd rather the skinflints have some cash left to offer Ellen. She's got the hard job, holding school for those scarecrow farm kids."

"They don't pay her much, either," Joe pointed out. "And there's less kids on the farms every week."

"Oh?"

"That Mills fellow's buyin' up land like there was no tomorrow. You know he bought out Alf Lovell. Now he's taken over the Humphrey place, the Jennings farm, a couple o' others."

"Ellen didn't say anything about that," Willie said, scratching his ear. "Wonder why."

"You ask me, she ain't had much chance to say anything to you the last couple o' weeks. You been out ridin' range mostly, or else keepin' office hours in town. Me, if I had a pretty widow lady givin' me a hopeful look, I'd find time to walk the river with her."

"We're not kids looking to start up a courtship."

"And you ain't so old and gray not to notice her," Joe said, grinning. "Skippin' breakfast and stayin' at that ole cabin up on the hill won't put her off forever, you know."

"I didn't know I was trying to put her off," Willie growled. "Just been busy."

"Sure," Joe said, laughing to himself. "Busy."

Willie didn't hold Joe's bemused grin against him. Even as the words rolled off Willie's lips, a growing hollowness inside him gave proof to the lie. How many cold, lonely nights had he lain awake thinking of her? How many dreams featured the two of them? And now, with her so near, he held back. Why?

He was still wondering when she returned from Esperanza that afternoon. It was always a sight to see: Ellen in her wool skirt and schoolmarmish cloak, driving the open-bed wagon full of wrestling youngsters homeward. Billy and his yellow-haired brothers, Cobb and Ellis, hopped out to tend the horses. Little Anne, whose walnut hair and turned-up nose brought a picture of her father to Willie's mind, climbed down from beside her mother and eyed her three brothers with wary six-year-old eyes.

"I see you brought in the cattle," Ellen called, as she ushered Anne toward the house. "You didn't spy any rustlers then."

"Not a one," Willie replied. "Just a pair of cowboys."

12

"They rode through town," she added. "Ray Rucker's boys."

"That's right."

"You didn't tell them who you were, did you? You wrote me about Ray, remember? You might at least have asked those two to supper."

"They didn't need reminders of their father," Willie grumbled. "And it's better not everyone knows just exactly who I am."

"You can't still be worried about Sam. You haven't seen him in close to fifteen years. He thinks you're dead."

"He did his best to make it that way, Ellie. And if somebody tells him different, he might hire it done a second time."

"And he might have forgotten all about whatever grudge he had against you."

"Sam Delamer never forgot anything. And neither have I. No, I don't want another war to fight. Best I stay Wil Fletcher."

"You'd know best about that," she said, opening the door for Anne.

"Well, you mean I win an argument for once?" he asked, bending over and lifting Anne's chin. "Hear that, Annie? Your mama's given me the last word."

"She must be tired," Billy said, as he swept past them into the house. "Too many school lessons, if you ask me."

Ellen gave a backward glance to where Ellis and Cobb were leading the horses into the barn.

"William Trent, you've got chores undone!" she called, scowling.

"Mama, Cobb's got it all in hand," Billy answered as he grabbed an ax. "I'm working on the woodpile. Was expecting somebody else to split firewood, but then I guess he was out riding all day."

"Sounds to me like somebody's growing a mite big for his britches," Willie said, blocking Billy's path to the door. "What do you think, son?"

"I think there's a storm brewing up over Blood Mesa that looks like it'll bury us in snow," the ten-year-old answered. "Look yourself. We'll need plenty of wood."

Willie allowed the youngster to hurry along, then stepped out to stare at the northern horizon.

"Lord help us," he muttered.

The same fool farmer who had christened the odd assortment of ramshackle huts in the middle of forlorn prairie grass "Esperanza" had also named the broken ridge north of Salt Fork Crossing "Blood Mesa." Old-timers said Comanches had massacred a family of settlers there, though nobody knew for sure. One thing was certain: At dawn and dusk, the mountain was painted bloodred by the rising and setting sun, and it was a haunted place to ride by night.

"Got its share o' haunts," Joe announced after an autumn deer hunt. "I got no love for such places. Bad things happen there."

"That's just superstition," Willie argued. "Good hunting in the thickets."

"Not good enough to pass another night here, Major. I'll find a better place tomorrow."

Just then, with thunderheads building overhead, there was a gray tint to the place. And as the wind begin to howl, Willie tasted rain—or worse.

"Yup," Joe called, as he led his horse toward the barn. "Snow. We'll be stayin' here, eh?"

"Could use the company, Uncle Wil!" Billy shouted from the woodpile.

"See to my horse," Willie answered. Then he stepped back inside to fetch a second ax.

For close to an hour Willie swung a heavy ax against juniper and willow logs, splitting and splintering them into stove wood. A short distance away Billy did likewise. They never exchanged a word, but the sharing of the chore drew the two of them together in a strange, silent way. Willie would pause and wipe sweat from his forehead, then glance over to see Billy do the same.

Each nodded to the other.

"You two share more than a name," Ellen had said often. It was a rare truth.

Outside the barn Ellis and Cobb plucked a pair of chickens that would become supper. Joe helped little Anne fill the water barrels, while Ellen latched the shutters. Already the wind had grown shrill, and there was an icy bite to the air.

The snowflakes started falling a few minutes later.

The first ones were soft, delicate things. They were followed by clumps of icy mush. Then the air turned white as a cloud of them tumbled earthward.

"Get inside!" Willie shouted, as he scrambled to collect the wood slivers.

Cobb and Ellis grabbed their plucked birds and raced for the door. Joe carried a water bucket in one arm and brought Anne along in the other. Ellen fastened the last of the shutters and then followed. Willie and Billy saw them all safely inside, then brought along a final armload of stove wood.

"Regular norther!" Ellen cried, as she rubbed snow out of her eyes. "Hurry, children, and shed those wet things. Get up close to the fire there, Ellis. No need to tempt Providence by catching your death."

Willie filled the woodbox before throwing off his damp coat and pulling off his boots. Joe saw to the water barrel before shedding wet buckskins behind the cover of the stove.

"Now this is real family living," Billy declared, when he pulled off his shirt and nudged Willie in the side.

"A little too real, to my thinking," Ellen announced, as she strung a line across the room and hung blankets to form a makeshift fence. "Boys on one side. We women on the other."

"Seems a pure waste," Cobb mumbled. "We all been swimming together."

15

"Not *all* of us!" Ellen amended.

"Well, not lately anyhow," Willie said, grinning.

"Mama, I hear a tale coming on," Billy said with a devilish grin. "You telling, or is Uncle Wil?"

"Neither," she answered, as she wrapped a warm shawl around her shoulders. "I've got chickens to bake, and you have lessons."

And so it was later, after supper, that they gathered around the fire to swap tales. Joe began with a story of wintering in the Spanish peaks, and Ellen spoke of her first winter in Kansas. When they'd finished, Cobb turned to Willie, pleading with his serious, nine-year-old eyes for a yarn.

"I'm cold," Ellis complained, huddling against his mother's side.

"Me too!" Anne cried, as she climbed onto Joe's lap.

"Ever remember being this cold?" Billy asked, as he and Cobb squeezed into the hollow between Willie and their mother. "Huh, Uncle Wil?"

"Cold?" he asked, as he felt Cobb's shoulder burrow into his side. "This isn't so cold."

"Tell us!" Cobb begged.

"Up in the Purgatory country this would pass for summer," Willie told them. "But the coldest I ever been was up in Virginia, the winter of '64 to '65, with Grant's Yankees hemming us in at Petersburg."

"Uncle Trav said you had to eat your own horses," Cobb said. "And men froze solid walking picket detail."

"Men froze," Willie agreed, as the memory engulfed him. "I woke up once to see a band of Yanks coming. Took out my rifle and aimed, but the hammer was frozen solid. I couldn't cock her. Yanks drew down on me, but their rifles weren't any better. We stood there looking at each other, not ten feet away. Then a bluecoat colonel took to shouting and waving his hands around. But his soldiers were helpless. One of our boys finally got a pistol shot off, and the whole attack turned tail. Raised a storm

16

of snow dust. In minutes they were white ghosts—just shadows."

"Tell us more!" Billy pleaded.

"Those aren't times dear to my heart, boys," Willie explained. "There were about fifty in our company when we were unhorsed and sent to the trenches. Fifteen or twenty saw spring, and less than that ever got home. Was at Five Forks we fought our last battle. There we were, running like crazy to get clear of Grant's army and the ghosts of Petersburg, when the whole Yank cavalry fell onto us. We stood and fought 'em the best we could. Travis, myself, a few others shot up a Yank column and got ourselves mounted. For just a while it seemed like we'd turned the fortunes of war. Then we realized there wasn't anybody else—just us and a hundred thousand Yankees. We skedaddled proper."

"And General Lee surrendered," Cobb added. "We know that from school."

"Yeah, Grant had the army in a box," Willie confessed. "But the Comanche cavalry, as we called ourselves, was still loose. I aimed to continue the fight, till I heard Lee called it quits. Wasn't anything left to do but turn for home."

"You never surrendered?" Ellen asked in surprise.

"Didn't sign any paper," Willie said, laughing. "I guess we didn't think the Union much cared about a handful of Texans. If we'd gone in to see Grant, he'd surely have kept our horses. They had U.S. brands, you see. And likely our rifles, too. Truth is, my old gray hat's about the only stitch of Confederate issue I had, then or now. And we were less than popular with those Michigan boys we rode down at the Forks. Wouldn't want to cross trails with them again."

"But that was April," Billy complained. "It wasn't cold then."

"There's different kinds of cold," Willie explained, as Cobb crawled up one knee. "Sure, it's cold outside now, but we got a warm fire and full bellies. Good company, too.

There's worse colds. Being all hollowed out empty, 'cause you've seen your best friends shot dead. Not knowing if your family's alive or dead. Having to leave all you know behind you and setting off into new country.''

"That's how it was leaving Kansas," Billy said. "And when Papa got shot."

"That's an icier cold than any norther ever brought," Willie observed.

Ellen gathered her brood to her side then, and they silently wept a moment. Then she announced it was time for bed, and the children spread out blankets around the stove and tried to find their rest.

"Long as I live, I'll never get the chill of those times out of my bones," Willie told Ellen later, as they sat beside the stove and watched the faint glimmer from the stove illuminate the sleeping heads of the little ones.

"At least you've spoken of it," she replied. "You haven't often talked about the war. Not to me, anyway."

"I've known better times."

"And worse?"

"Yes," he admitted. "But there's comfort in company."

"Oh?"

"I never forgot you, Ellie. Not on the darkest winter night. Nor nigh frozen in the high country."

"Nor I you. And now I need you."

"I'm here."

"Part of you. You would protect us. Help us. But we all of us need more. Want more. Those little ones hunger for a father."

"They've had one. Jack was a better man than I could be. I'd disappoint them. And you."

"Don't you think you're selling yourself short?"

"I know me better than you do. Besides, Jack's not been dead a year yet. It's judged proper to wait a bit."

"How long?"

"At least a year."

"A year," she said, shaking her head. "A year? I've

waited fifteen, Willie! It was 1865 you were supposed to come home to me.''

"Home? Where's that?"

"Home's anyplace you choose it to be. Don't you know that by now?"

"I've heard people say that, but I don't altogether think it's so. Up in the Big Horn country an old Sioux medicine chief told me I'd find peace if I went back where I lost myself. Trouble is, I've left bits and pieces of me all over. I figured peace waited in Texas, but it hasn't come."

"Isn't this peace?" she asked, clutching his arm. "Don't you see it, feel it? Aren't we enough?"

"I don't know, Ellie."

"Then I'm woeful sorry for you, Willie Delamer. Because you've lost more than a man's likely to find."

"I know," he agreed. "I know."

CHAPTER 3

Ice and snow melt. Life goes on. So it had always been, Willie told himself when the blizzard spent itself, and he helped Billy and Cobb harness the horses for the morning journey into town.

"Seems to me a thaw's a good excuse for a school holiday," Billy remarked. "Course, Mama doesn't see it that way."

"She's got your best interests at heart," Willie declared. "Wouldn't want you to turn out ignorant like me."

"You read well enough, and even Mama admits you do passable good with your numbers," Billy argued. "You didn't go to school, I bet."

"Not like you do, maybe, but my mama had me at lessons often enough. And I had schooling of a sort elsewhere," Willie explained.

"Yeah?" Cobb asked.

"Learned to gentle horses and hunt buffalo, riding with the Comanches. Papa taught me the cattle trade. And later, I picked up soldiering from one sergeant or another."

"You were a major," Billy pointed out. "How'd a sergeant teach you?"

"I didn't start out an officer," Willie said, frowning.

"Didn't want to be one, in fact. Isn't easy, leading men. But by and by the others fell, and the men looked to me."

"That's how it was for Papa," Billy declared. "He was a doctor, and they looked up to him. They expected him to speak up about things. Got him killed."

"Trouble with being a leader is that it makes it hard for a man to back down," Willie told the youngsters. "And there was no back-stepping in your papa. It grieves me I didn't know him better."

"He liked you a lot," Billy announced. "Told Cobb and me once to stick tight to you if we ever got in a fix and he wasn't around."

"Did he?"

"Yes, sir," Cobb agreed. "We done it, too."

"Well, won't be too much longer you'll need somebody to lean on, boys. Growing taller every day, the both of you."

"We got a long time," Billy asserted. "Years. Even you didn't go to war till you were fifteen."

"You know all about that, do you?" Willie asked, as he finished hitching the horses to the wagon.

"Mama told us," Cobb explained. "She tells fine stories of the old days. Yours are more exciting, though. She doesn't talk wild Indians or buffalo."

"She recalls the better times," Willie muttered. "That's a gift."

As was his custom when not rounding up stray cows, Willie accompanied Ellen and the children to Esperanza. He was, after all, town marshal. True, Esperanza was just a huddle of buildings, and its biggest crimes consisted of boys snatching apples off Rupe Hamer's mercantile counter. Even so, Willie made a point of thumbing through the various wanted posters and telegrams that came via the county seat or were delivered by the rangers up from Albany.

It was rarely dull, that ride to town. Billy, Cobb, and Ellis were ever ready with some new prank, usually aimed at their mother or little sister, and Willie often found himself enforcing one of Ellen's laws behind the cover of a gnarled oak.

"Nothing like a good switching to drive the Devil out of a boy," Elizabeth Delamer had taught her son. Willie was never better than a halfhearted believer in the adage, though, and the youngsters all knew he lacked their mama's enthusiasm for such chastisement.

"You got to be part Cheyenne," Joe once remarked. "White men are hard on their kids. They rub all the shine from their eyes."

"Not all of them do," Willie complained.

"No? Watch how they break a horse to saddle. They work their boys the same way. See if it ain't true, Major. Just look and see if it ain't!"

It wasn't possible to argue with Joe Eagle about such things. He saw with a truth. Pain and death had cleared his sight, and he didn't mince his words.

Fortunately, that morning Willie had already freed the frog Cobb had stashed in his own lunch pail, and thus the boys' tormenting of Anne was foiled. Moreover, Cobb eyed Willie guiltily, and the three boys were on their best behavior lest the story make its way to Ellen's ears.

Once they arrived in town, Willie paused at the schoolhouse while Ellen and the children went about their duties. Billy helped unhitch the horses, and the animals were left to graze out back. Afterward Willie rode along to the jail house, tied his horse to a hitching post outside, and set about going through the latest batch of posters left by the midweek stage.

"Any real desperadoes in the bunch?" Rupert Hamer asked, as he stepped inside the narrow room that served as marshal's office.

"Here's a fellow after your heart, Rupe," Willie said, tossing a poster toward the shopkeeper.

"Says here he's wanted for bigamy," Hamer said, laughing. "Has seven different wives! Lord, I wonder how they caught up with him."

"Got his picture in the paper down in Austin," Willie explained. "Now he's really famous."

"Favored bankers' daughters, too. Was good money in it. Best I not let Dewey hear of this. He's forever scheming to pick up some easy money."

"That's a boy you won't hear any cross words from me about," Willie said. "You get tired of having him for a nephew, let me know. I'll take him in."

"You may have to. He's got a better head for trading horses than minding a counter. I judge you've spoiled him for honest work, Major."

"Boy's just got a feel for open country."

"Like others I've known," Hamer added. "When are you going to give up that addled notion of ranching on Salt Fork and come to town and settle down?"

"On ten dollars a month?"

"I could get you a fair raise, Wil. Or run you against old Murdock for sheriff."

"Then I'd be forever in Throckmorton!"

"We could move the county seat."

"To a town of twenty people?" Willie asked, laughing. "Not a prayer. Truth is, if anybody else leaves Esperanza, there won't be any town."

"Maybe, maybe not. This Mills fellow's got plans. Before long he'll have himself a big spread. Ranch that size needs a town nearby to serve it."

"Grass hereabouts is fine for buffalo and a few beeves, but it'll take lots of acres to run a big herd. And don't forget, the water's mostly on my land."

"I doubt that's gone by Mills without notice, Major. He'll be buying you out next. You and Ellen Trent."

"Make us both rich, huh?" Willie asked, laughing at the notion.

"He's being plenty generous, Wil," Hamer said, turning serious. "Purchased my brother Simon's farm. Sime's off to California, and I'm considering it myself."

"If Sime's gone west, then Dewey . . ."

"Is living with me at the store. He's my worry, remember? Anyhow, he's sixteen now, and too old for you to be worrying over. You have enough stray pups to bother with at Salt Fork Crossing."

"I don't—"

"Give it up, man. Any fool can see the way the Trent boys take to you. Dewey, too. You're a softer man than you like to credit yourself. Lord only knows why you don't get on and marry Ellen Trent. She's a lovely soul who's in need of a bit of tenderness, and I don't believe she'd have anyone else."

"We're just old friends."

"The best kind," Hamer said, grinning.

A knock on the door halted their conversation.

"Am I interrupting anything?" a tall, middle-aged man dressed in a brown tailored suit asked.

"How are you, Mr. Mills?" Hamer asked. "We were just the two of us talking about you. Wil, this is Abner Mills in the flesh. Mr. Mills, meet Marshal Wil Fletcher."

"Welcome to Esperanza, Mr. Mills," Willie said, offering his hand. Mills gripped it firmly.

"I've come to judge a man by his grip, Fletcher," Mills declared. "Yours is rock-hard, but not overpowering. Confident. Good sign in a lawman."

"Not a lot of lawlessness in Esperanza," Willie pointed out. "Pretty quiet hereabouts."

"Glad to hear it. Come meet my family," Mills added.

He stepped aside so that his wife, a friendly, slight-figured blond woman in her mid-thirties, could wave their four youngsters inside the jail house.

"Marshal Fletcher, my wife Loretta," Mills said. "My eldest, Alice." A tall, yellow-haired girl of fifteen curtsied. "My boys, Albert, Jacob, and Jonathan."

Albert, thirteen, offered his hand. Jacob, smaller and frail to a fault at eleven, sheltered eight-year-old Jonathan behind their mother.

"Jake doesn't much take to strangers," Albert explained.

"Leastwise, not ugly ones like me," Willie said, winking at the boy. "You've a fine family, Mr. Mills. So, what is it I can do for you?"

"Mainly wanted to meet the local law," Mills explained. "Then, too, I heard you own a good lot of acreage along the Salt Fork. In fact, the cattle-crossing on the trail to Dodge City."

"Lots of places to cross Salt Fork in normal times," Willie replied. "The place folks think of as the main crossing actually belongs to a friend of mine. Ellen Trent. She's also the schoolteacher here in Esperanza."

"Ah, I remember now," Mills said, scratching his chin. "Widow of the town doctor. Shame about that. If we had come out sooner, that unpleasantness might have been avoided. You'll find I'm quite good at settling disputes before they get out of hand."

"Pa's ranched down south in Webb County," Albert boasted. "Before he got down there the Mexicans used to steal a lot of cows. You put an end to that, didn't you, Pa?"

"I did indeed," Mills said, hooking his thumbs in his side pockets and standing tall. "You'll find me a rock of law and order, Marshal. A rock."

"I'm pleased to hear it," Willie said halfheartedly. "We don't have many Mexicans come through here, though. And the ones who do usually ride with trail herds headed for Kansas."

"But that isn't to say you don't suffer from rustling, is it?" Mills asked.

"No, sir, we've had some losses," Willie readily confessed. "Not any big number, but a few here and there."

"Any thought as to who is doing it? I understand there was a family of squatters here, the Scarlets."

"They're mostly dead, and the ones that aren't are far too young to trouble us."

"You're certain of that?" Mills asked.

"I just said it, didn't I?" Willie retorted somewhat heatedly.

25

Mills motioned his family outside, then stared at Hamer.

"I'll speak with you a bit later," Hamer said to Wil, turning to leave.

"Tell Dewey I've got a pair of colts need work out at my place," Willie replied. "He's welcome anytime."

"That won't encourage him to work any harder, you know," Hamer complained. "I'll tell him, though."

Mills shut the door behind Hamer, then turned on Willie with fiery eyes.

"Now look here, Fletcher, I've been civil enough to this point. I've been here three weeks now, and every time I turn around I have stock missing."

"With all these storms—"

"They're not being spooked by lightning! Nor falling into some ravine. Half the time we find butchered carcasses. We have range thieves afoot, and I expect an end to be put to them."

"I rode out with my deputy yesterday and had a look," Willie explained. "Didn't find a sign of what you're talking about."

"Maybe you didn't look hard enough," Mills growled. "Or maybe you didn't recognize rustlers when they stared you in the face."

"Meaning?"

"I heard of those two cowboys you let go. They rode through town afterward, grown fat on my steers."

"Best you know the whole story," Willie declared. "Joe and I found them nigh starved, let go in the deep of winter by old man Austin down in Hood County. Wasn't either of them hiding what they did. Nor proud of it. As to the steer, it bore no brand."

"You know the law sees a maverick as property of the landowner."

"I've heard that, though I understand it's ruled elsewise some. Anyway, it was my land they were camped on, so if the loss is anyone's it's mine."

"This time, maybe. And the next?"

"They're likely up north at their uncle's place by now. Lord, Mills, the youngest wasn't much older'n your Albert, and scarce any taller. Would you begrudge a couple of boys the beef to hold off starvation?"

"It's not that that rankles me."

"Then what is it?" Willie asked.

"You!" Mills stormed. "It's your duty to arrest skinners, or cow thieves, or whatever you look at them as being."

"Within the town limits of Esperanza," Willie declared. "That's where my jurisdiction begins and ends. You don't believe that, talk to the county sheriff, L. D. Murdock. He's quick to quote the law to me. I can scare off a hider or two, but I don't have much weight of law in my favor."

"Down around Laredo we hang thieves."

"Without a trial?" Willie asked. "On suspicion? You must run mighty shy of boys down that way. If your sons were out riding and they came across a lame cow, shot and skinned her, would you want somebody stringing them up first chance they got?"

"That's not what I'm suggesting."

"Isn't it? Look, Mills, I'll keep Esperanza nice and peaceful. And if you want, I'll look around your range now and then. But as to hanging strangers . . ."

"Don't you worry yourself over my place!" Mills barked. "I'll attend to this matter personally."

"See it's within the boundaries of the law," Willie warned.

"It will be," Mills promised. "Count on that!"

CHAPTER 4

"Don't let that Mills get your dander up," Ellen advised, as she drove the wagon home that afternoon.

"You should have heard the way he talked to me!" Willie exclaimed.

"I've got a pretty fair idea," she replied. "He and his prim wife marched into school and insisted everyone stop while they explained how they wish their children to be educated. You ask me, I ought to start with them. Once they left, though, things settled down. Alice is quite bright, and young Albert is sure to shine in mathematics."

"Jake's all right, too," Billy added. "Quiet, but he'll come around."

"Jonathan doesn't talk," Ellis declared. "He's sort of scared all the time."

"He's plain simple," Billy announced.

"Not at all," Ellen argued. "Last year he had a bad fright. His mother said some raiders tried to burn their house. One of them threatened Jonathan with a knife."

"The Scarlets like to kill us, Mama, but we aren't still scared," Billy grumbled.

"He's come to a strange place," Willie pointed out. "Doesn't know anybody much. That can be scary all by itself. Remember when you youngsters came here from Kansas.''

"We didn't have time to be scared," Billy complained. "Was too much work to do."

"And there still is!" Ellen cried. "I do want to make it clear there'll be no more talk of being simple. Clear?"

"Yes, ma'am," the children muttered.

"That's better," she added, as she slowed the wagon. Soon it rumbled to a stop beside the barn, and the boys scrambled out and set to unharnessing the horses.

For close to a week thereafter a rare spell of peace fell over Throckmorton County. No rustlers disturbed Abner Mills's cattle, and no more strangers crossed the Salt Fork. February was half gone now, and if it hadn't yet turned springtime warm the worst of winter seemed to be fading into memory.

"I'd almost pay a price to be alive on a day like this," Willie remarked to Joe Eagle one Tuesday morning.

"Be a bad bargain," Joe declared. "I smell rain."

Joe Eagle smelled trouble, too, and he spelled it out.

"River's too full to be safe," the Cheyenne explained. "Our cabin won't weather a flood, and the horses won't be safe, either."

"You sure?" Willie asked. "I set the cabin on yon hill. Water would have to rise three, four feet to bother it. And the horses . . ."

"I seen floods before, up on the Washita and along the Arkansas, both. There the ground'd mop up some o' the water. This sand won't soak up spit. Be a flood comin', Major."

Willie had traveled enough miles with Indians to trust them on such matters, so he set to moving his horses to higher ground right away. There was a good box canyon past Coon Hollow, and it wasn't hard to fence the entrance. Willie, Joe, and young Dewey Hamer had the rails in place an hour before the first cloudburst. And before the river left its banks, Joe and Willie dragged their belongings up a hill topped by oak trees a quarter mile from Ellen's place.

"River won't be content to take our cabin," Joe grumbled, as he pointed to the raging torrent that Salt Fork had become.

"Best I ride over and give Ellen a hand," Willie said, frowning. "That house was built solid, Joe."

"Won't last out this river," the Indian argued.

"Where will I take them? Can't little ones sleep out in the open."

"There's caves up Blood Mesa," Joe explained. "You go fetch 'em. I'll meet you there."

"I don't like that place much," Willie said uneasily.

"Only shelter shy o' town. Can't put up everybody in the jail."

"The school . . ."

"Would be good, only you figure we can get 'em there?"

Willie eyed the darkening skies and shook his head. In a flash he mounted a gray stallion and rode south toward Salt Fork Crossing.

Water was already lapping at the door when Willie arrived at the house. Ellen had the little ones sitting atop the heavy oak dining table, and possessions were securely tied to roof beams.

"We'll be all right," Ellen assured him, when Willie splashed his way inside. "I've known high water before. Don't forget, I grew up along the Brazos."

"Joe says this is just the beginning," Willie explained. "River might carry off the house. You willing to chance it?"

"Mama, Joe Eagle's generally right," Billy reminded her.

"Can we take anything with us?" Ellen asked.

"Only what you can carry," Willie answered. "Food and spare clothes. Blankets."

"Where are we going, Uncle Wil?" Cobb asked, as he climbed atop Willie's shoulders.

"Blood Mesa," Willie replied. "Joe's finding us a cave."

"I don't like that place," Cobb complained. "Joe says there's spirits there."

"It's haunted," Anne agreed.

Willie only shook his head and helped Cobb up onto the back of the big gray.

"How'll we get there?" Billy called.

"Billy, you and Ellis will ride old Cyrus," Willie said, indicating the broad-backed plow horse most accustomed to hauling freight in the open-bed wagon. "Ellen, you and Annie can ride Matilda," he added, noting the second horse.

"We got no saddles for 'em," Ellis complained.

"We'll tie some blankets on, then lash down your gear," Willie said, hurrying back to accept a bundle from Ellen. "I'll make a line of sorts for you to hold on to. Don't let go unless you plan to swim to the Gulf of Mexico."

"I'd rather not," Ellen said, trying to bolster the spirits of the children. It didn't work. Between the damp and the cold, they were already shivering.

"Better hurry, Uncle Wil," Billy said, jumping down from the table and splashing into ankle-deep water. "The river's rising."

"Sure is," Ellis agreed, struggling down beside his older brother.

"We better go," Ellen declared, as Annie climbed onto her shoulders. "It's getting worse."

Willie nodded. It was true. No sooner had he lashed down the gear and satisfied himself Ellen and the little ones were secure than the skies literally emptied themselves. Rain fell in torrents, and thunder shook the land. The children screamed, and the horses began to balk.

"Sooner you get going, you poor dumb creatures, the faster we get to Joe's cave," Willie chastised the beasts. He then climbed atop the gray, shuddering as the fierce wind lashed his face. Little Cobb clung to his back.

"Let's go," Willie called to the others. He gave a reassuring tap to Cobb's fingers, then led the way toward Blood Mesa.

It was a long ride under the worst possible circumstances. The wind and the wet and the cold combined to plague the little band. From time to time the children whimpered and moaned. Those sounds tore at Willie, and he wished he had something to fend off the torrent. Ellen's attempts at comfort were swallowed by the howling wind.

"Not much farther," Willie told them again and again. But the going was slow, what with creeks swelling and the ground turning into a quagmire. And anyway, there was no cure for fright.

In an hour's time they had crossed better than two miles of soggy plain, and Blood Mesa loomed near. By then Willie himself was half-frozen and wet through to the bone. He felt Cobb's shivering fingers claw his back and knew the others were cold as well. He swallowed a sob as he recalled how light Anne had rested on his shoulders a few days before.

Up ahead the haunted mountain finally emerged from gray mists. A pinprick of light broke through the haze, and Willie turned in that direction.

"Joe'll have a fire going!" Billy cried, as he swung old Cyrus in line.

"Thank the Lord for that," Ellen added, as she followed.

Willie wove his way up a steep slope toward the light. He got to within a hundred yards before the gray balked. Looking back, he saw the draft horses had halted some distance below. The last quarter mile would require mountain-goat feet.

"We're about there," Willie called, as he dismounted. Cobb rolled off the saddle and fell against Willie's side. A wet bundle of old rags would have shown more life. Willie eased the boy onto one shoulder and trudged up the hill to the cave.

The trail was little more than a foot tracing in the sandstone ridge, and Willie slipped a dozen times. Each time little Cobb groaned and shuddered, but the boy voiced no complaint.

"Joe?" Willie called, when he finally reached the narrow mouth of the cave.

"About to give you up," Joe answered, as he rushed over. The Indian helped slide Cobb off Willie's muddy shoulder, then stared warily down the slope.

"Tend him," Willie said, shaking water from his coat. "I'm going for the others."

Joe started to argue, but Willie was already in motion. He was quickly outside, into the storm once more.

He slipped and floundered downhill to where Billy had managed to drag Ellis. Ellen and Anne remained a hundred yards behind with the bundled belongings.

"I got the horses unpacked," a weary Billy explained. "Let 'em go, Uncle Wil. They were done in."

"They'll find their own shelter," Willie agreed, noting the gray had vanished as well. "Can you make it up the hill?"

"Don't know," Billy said, his knees giving way as he leaned on Willie's shoulder.

"Get under those junipers there," Willie instructed. "Best I see to Annie."

Billy nodded, then nudged Ellis along to where a pair of gnarled trees provided a windbreak of sorts. Willie headed on to the others. After nodding to Ellen, he threw the clothes and food bundles over his left shoulder, took Anne in his strong right arm, and began the tortuous climb back to the cave.

His mind drifted as he wove his way up the slippery path. Once or twice he half faltered, but Anne squeezed his arm with her little hands and that spurred him on. He finally reached the cave, turned the girl over to Joe, and laid the soggy possessions beside the fire.

"Best I make the next trip," Joe argued.

"Look after the little ones," Willie countered. "I'm gone."

Meanwhile Ellen had managed somehow to reach Billy and Ellis. The three of them were struggling up the narrow path together, and Willie met them a hundred yards from the cave's mouth. The light and its promise of a warm fire filled the four of them with new resolve, and though Willie had to half drag the boys the rest of the way, they all staggered inside the cave in time.

"Cozy up to that fire!" Joe barked as he pulled Ellis off Willie's shoulder. "Once you warm a hair, get shed o' your clothes. I got horse blankets you can use till your duds dry."

Willie wearily kicked off his boots and threw off his coat. Already it felt as if an iron anvil were sitting atop his chest, and the chill was spreading through him like a summer prairie fire.

"Here," Joe said, offering Willie a cup of boiling coffee. "Get to the fire."

"The others . . ." Willie muttered.

Joe laughed a second, then turned to offer Ellen a cup as well. Her motherly instinct had taken hold, though, and she was occupying herself looking after the children.

"You all right, Uncle Wil?" Cobb called from the fire.

Willie tried to manage an answer, but his fingers grew numb and he tottered onto his side. The world went black.

When Willie's eyes regained their focus, he saw Ellen and the little ones huddled beside a roaring fire, their soggy hair and weary eyes attesting to the ordeal. They were a sight, wrapped in saddle blankets, their bare toes stretched toward the red coals. Joe Eagle was at work rubbing moisture from his back.

"Told you he'd come around," Billy told his brothers. "Uncle Wil's known lots of worse times'n this."

"Carried Anne and me all the way up this hill," Cobb boasted, hugging his sister closer. "Was near froze, wasn't he, Annie?"

"Just about an icicle," the girl added. "Wet, too."

34

"Miz Trent, try another cup o' that coffee on him," Joe suggested. "Ain't so bad he'd pass out twice."

Ellen grinned, poured coffee into a tin cup, and handed it to Billy. The ten-year-old scrambled over with the boiling liquid.

"Warms a body some," Billy said, as he held the cup to Willie's cracked lips. He sipped the coffee, then nodded as the warmth flowed back into his chest.

"Thanks," Willie said, as Billy settled in at his side. "Another minute and I might have been Annie's icicle."

"We might all've been," Ellen declared. "If we hadn't drowned. I'll bet the river's ten feet over its banks."

"Closer to twenty," Joe said, as he wrapped a blanket tightly over Willie's shoulders. "Be half a week 'fore we get off this hill."

"I can't stay here that long," Ellen objected. "There's the school. . . ."

"Nobody's goin' nowhere anytime soon," Joe argued. " 'Cept maybe swimmin'."

"Too cold!" Ellis cried, shivering.

"Floods pass," Willie declared. He sipped the rest of the coffee, then set the cup aside. "Spring'll happen along, and you'll wish you had some of this cool night again."

"That's the trouble with Texas," Billy complained. "It's too hot or too cold."

"Too wet or too dry," Cobb added.

"Now who ever told you that?" Willie asked, laughing as their fingers pointed to him. "Ellie, you think you can find something to feed us that's not waterlogged?"

"I can," she answered, turning to the food bundles.

And so they circled the fire and chewed cold beef and biscuits. Another time it might have been a moment of true misery, but sitting there, sharing the warmth of the fire and the comfort of Ellen's warm smile, with the children's tired arms draped over his shoulders, Willie felt the cold flow out of him.

After eating, they hung wet clothes on poles beside the

fire and laughed at each other's soggy hair and pale skin.

"I seen plucked chickens with more hide on 'em," Billy told Cobb.

"And I passed a scarecrow with more color," Cobb retorted.

The boys wrestled a few minutes, alternately laughing and howling. It drew Willie back twenty years, to a time when he and Ellen's brother Travis had passed a winter's night in a Brazos cave back in Palo Pinto County.

"Remembering?" Ellen whispered.

"Yes," Willie confessed. As he told her of the adventure, the children gathered close. The story seemed to restore their spirits.

"We were just fine till the wolf came," Willie said, feeling the little ones cling closer to their mother. "Big old wolf it was, too, gray as dust, with teeth like razors. Trav and I watched that old thing come creeping up on us, and we just about had a fit.

" 'What'll we do?' he asked me, and I was hanged if I knew. Then I remembered something old Yellow Shirt, the Comanche chief, told me once. You run into trouble, state your business and don't show fear. So I eyed that wolf and said, 'Wolf, we don't mean you any harm. How were we to know this was your house? We'll get along come morning, and you'll be no worse for it.' "

"And the wolf let you stay?" Billy asked.

"Nope," Willie answered, waiting for the children to grow close.

"Then what happened?" Cobb demanded.

"Why, that wolf went and gobbled us up," Willie said, grabbing the four of them and making a gnashing sound. The children shrieked and struggled, then broke out laughing.

"Trav told me about that time," Ellen said, as she separated the tangled arms and legs of the youngsters. "There really was a wolf."

"But he didn't eat you," Billy pointed out.

"No, he left us to ourselves," Willie confessed. "Old Yellow Shirt's advice was sound. Always was, in fact."

"Indians know things," Joe boasted, nodding his head and giving them a solemn frown.

"Know about rain, anyhow," Billy agreed. "But the warning could've come earlier."

"Well, I been a time ridin' the white man's road," Joe explained. "Waters down my powers."

"Yeah?" Willie asked. "Maybe you'd better head on up to the Nations, huh?"

"And eat salt beef and listen to old women's stories?" Joe cried. "No, I'll take my chances with Texas floods and yellow-haired demons."

"We'd miss you if you went anywhere," Anne said, creeping over and resting her head in Joe's lap. "You, too, Uncle Wil."

"Guess I'd miss you some, too, little gal," Willie admitted.

"There's a solution to that," Ellen said, gazing deeply into his eyes.

"Yeah," Billy agreed. "We could use a new papa."

Five sets of eyes fixed on his face, but Willie only looked away.

"There's a house to rebuild, and animals to round up," he told them. "Other affairs can wait."

CHAPTER 5

The rains continued to plague Texas that hard winter, and the Salt Fork flooded miles and miles of range. Stranded cows and horses gazed hungrily from island ridges, while their owners waited helplessly for the flood waters to recede.

Willie occupied his time tending to the needs of Ellen and the youngsters. When not hunting up fresh meat, he would gather them close and share a tale of better days. One moment he would be racing horses with painted Indians, the next he was digging gold from distant streambeds.

In time the rains abated, and the river returned to its banks. It was then possible to assess the damage and learn the grim truth. Only a stone wall remained to mark Salt Fork Crossing. Of the house and barn there was nothing. Downstream Willie located a cedar chest and a bed frame. Otherwise it was as if the place had been erased from the earth.

Elsewhere in Throckmorton County, much the same story was being told. In that hot, dry country, farmers located their homes near a dependable source of water—namely, the Salt Fork. And so the flood had carried off the log and plank houses with a willful disregard for their inhabitants. Worse, here and there a child had been swept away, swallowed by the demon river. The Blantons, an elderly couple of Iowans, had perished when their cabin had collapsed.

"Two families out of three are ruined," Prudence Gunnerson told Willie when she visited the crossing. "And even among those who aren't, there's a feeling of great despair. It's as if the Lord's turned against us."

"Ma'am, it's just Texas, is all," Willie told the old woman. "We've known worse."

"We have," she agreed. "But many of us were younger then. I've just got my grandsons to live for now, you know. I grow tired easy. Abner Mills has offered me a handsome price for my farm."

"Plan to take it?" Willie asked.

"I've thought on it, but people look to me for strength."

Willie nodded. It was Granny Gunnerson who had brought the Trents down from Kansas, who had led her little army of Iowa widows and war orphans to Texas in hopes of making a fresh start. They had fought hard to hold onto their homes, those Iowans. But now they were beaten.

It showed in their faces.

"I used to find comfort in the name of our town," Granny Gunnerson said, dabbing her eyes with a linen handkerchief. "Esperanza. It means 'hope' in Spanish."

"I know, ma'am," Willie said, nodding sadly.

"But hope's come to an end, hasn't it?"

"Oh, there's never an end to hope," he argued. "Better times are sure to come along."

"But not for us," the old woman added with a sigh.

Two days later Rupert Hamer passed along word of Prudence Gunnerson's surrender.

"She's sold her place to Mills," Hamer explained. "Gone to California, like Simon. As if there's any pot of gold awaiting them there!"

"Well, this never was farm country," Willie muttered. "I wish 'em luck. They had little enough of it here."

"I brought some better news, too," Hamer went on. "Dewey's waiting downriver a mile or so. There's a bend there where a regular pile of planks is waiting. I'll bet three, four farmhouses washed up there. You'd never know those planks were ever nailed to one another, but they could be. I thought you might like to take your wagon down and fetch them along. We'd lend a hand rebuilding the place."

"Ellen'd appreciate that," Willie replied. "We'll get started right now."

"I'm a fair hand with a hammer," Hamer added. "I could build some chests, frame the windows. . . ."

"I don't have money to pay you, but . . ."

"Was I asking any?" Hamer cried. "Don't you figure I owe you for what you did when those Scarlets had at us? And for the time you've offered Dewey?"

"That was freely given," Willie explained.

"And so is this," Hamer responded. "Now, are we going to get that wagon ready or not?"

With Rupe and Dewey Hamer helping, Willie and Joe hauled four loads of planks to Salt Fork Crossing. Some were terribly broken, and many had twisted nails jutting wickedly from their ends. Most were salvageable, though, and Dewey even managed to save some of the nails. What else was needed Rupe ordered from Albany on the telegraph, and by the end of the month the house was taking shape.

"We put the house and barn both up in one day before," Willie lamented, as he splintered cedar logs into shingles.

"Had most of the county to help, too," Hamer pointed out. "People were awful eager to have school start, and they were anxious for the doctor to get settled, too."

"Everybody's busy now," young Dewey declared, as he swept a handful of thick blond hair from his forehead.

"They were busy then," Willie grumbled. "They've got no eagerness to help a man who can't dose their little ones or birth babies. I would've thought they'd lend Ellen a hand, though."

"Or show you some gratitude for what you did last fall," Dewey added. "People have short memories."

"It's not that," Hamer objected. "It's just, well, they've got other worries. Some are trying to organize a stock auction. Others are settling accounts and heading west. It's not they don't remember. They've simply got other business pressing."

"Abner Mills is sendin' his boys to Miz Trent for schoolin'," Dewey said, scowling. "And he's hired plenty of new men. He could spare some of them to help."

"Mills ain't about to help anybody save himself," Joe barked. "I seen men like him plenty o' times. If it ain't his roof, he don't care if it burns. If it ain't his cow, let the flood have it. Yessir, he's got white man's sickness mighty bad. Only got love o' greenbacks and gold pieces."

"You're judging him awfully hard," Ellen said as she brought a water bucket by. "He sent all the way to St. Louis for schoolbooks."

"The kind he wanted you to use," Willie muttered. "Am I right?"

"He did have a text in mind, but . . ."

"Man like that's got cash handy to win an argument sure enough," Willie declared. "But I don't know I'd chalk that up to generosity."

"Nor'd I," Hamer agreed with a laugh. "Still, he's paid an honest dollar for the land he's bought. Could've had it for half the sum, most times. And he's bent nobody's arm, either."

"Hasn't had to," Dewey said, as he strained to help his uncle set a window frame in place.

Gradually the house was built, and Ellen deemed it her duty to resume her responsibilities at the school.

"Best I stay and help Uncle Wil with the shingling," Billy said, when it was time to leave that next morning.

"Best you do what your mama says," Willie argued. "Leave the shingles to Joe and me."

"You heard him," Ellen said, grinning. "Into the wagon, William!"

"Ah, Mama, don't you figure I've got enough schooling to last me?" the boy asked. "I'm closing in on eleven, after all."

"The wagon," Ellen said sternly, and Billy followed her pointing finger.

Once Ellen and the children had left, Willie climbed the east wall and started nailing shingles in place. For once the wind was light, and the morning sun had managed to chase the March chill northward.

"Seems to me you'd save yourself a lot o' worry if you put together a skin lodge," Joe complained, as he joined Willie atop the roof. "Ever see a tipi floatin' down a river?"

"That and worse," Willie said, shaking his head. "Forgetting I was on Powder River back in March of '76, when Crook's army hit the Cheyennes and Sioux? Lord, that was just four years ago!"

"No cavalry to burn your tipi hereabouts," Joe pointed out, sighing.

"Maybe not, but plenty of hard hearts where Indians are concerned. Don't tell me you haven't noticed them."

"Confess I've seen 'em," Joe admitted. "Still . . ."

"It's not my house anyway," Willie pointed out. "I'd build her one of those big white houses with the columns in front and the tall windows . . . if it was what she wanted. She hasn't had an easy going, Joe. Deserves better."

"You'll see she has what she needs."

"Wish I had the power," Willie mumbled. "Never have had before."

Joe started to speak, then swallowed the words. Instead he pointed toward the river. A dark column of smoke was rising skyward a mile past the crossing, and Willie tensed. Then, as the wind gusted, he heard the sound of gunshots.

"Major, that ain't our business," Joe argued, as Willie started down the side of the house.

42

"Still got myself a badge, don't I?" Willie asked. "And anyway, I own that stretch along the river."

"Might be on past there," Joe said, swinging off the eaves and dropping to the ground. "Got the horses off west o' there now."

"Coming?" Willie asked, as he buckled on his pistol belt and headed for the big gray.

"You know I am," Joe grumbled. "Ain't a smart thing, but no wise Cheyenne'd join up with a crazy man in the first place."

Willie laughed as he saddled his stallion. Then, after sliding a Winchester into a saddle scabbard, he climbed atop the anxious horse. Joe had already mounted his pinto, and the two of them splashed across the still deep river and headed north toward the gunfire.

They galloped close to half a mile before slowing. Willie's gray snorted and stomped, and he halted the big animal.

"Easy, boy," Willie whispered, sniffing the air. He, too, picked up the scent of powder.

"I got the right," Joe said, turning that way.

"Then I got the left," Willie replied. They then continued cautiously up a slight slope, turned east as the river made a bend, and came upon a small party of horsemen prowling beyond what had been a camp of sorts alongside Salt Fork.

"Good Lord!" Willie cried, as he stared at three lumps on the sandy ground beside a smoldering campfire.

"Well, if it isn't our marshal!" Abner Mills shouted, turning to greet the new arrivals. "Marshal Fletcher, welcome to the party!"

The seven horsemen behind him raised a scornful hoot, and Mills laughed out loud.

"Morning, Mr. Mills," Willie called, swallowing an urge to lash out.

"Marshal, if I'd known you were patrolling the river, I might have left this little chore to you," Mills said, pointing to a fourth body slumped across a boulder. "Told you there were rustlers about."

"Oh?" Willie asked.

"I don't see nothin' stolen," Joe added, as he dismounted. "No hides nor nothin', Major."

"We had fifty head run off," Mills insisted. "Followed the tracks to here."

"And I'm certain you talked to these fellows," Willie said, hatefully eyeing the grinning cowboys. "Told you to take your complaints up with the county sheriff in Throckmorton."

"Did better'n that," Mills said, laughing. "Brought the sheriff to the trouble. Don't suppose you've met our new sheriff, have you? Here he is now."

A tall, dark-haired rider with cold eyes and a grim stare nudged his horse into a trot and rode toward Willie.

"Name's Livingston," the new sheriff said, nodding toward his badge.

"Thurman's been with the Rangers down south," Mills explained.

"What became of Murdock?" Willie asked.

"I persuaded him the job required a younger man," Mills said, laughing.

"Mr. Mills has a way with words," Livingston added. "He mostly wins his arguments."

"So I see," Willie muttered, as he glanced at the corpses. Not a one of them looked past twenty, and the one closest to the fire couldn't have been more than fifteen.

"Just boys," Joe declared, as he turned the nearest onto his back. "Lord, Major, we seen this one before."

"On his birthday," Willie said, shuddering at the sight of Polk Rucker's lifeless face. The young man's chest had been blown apart by rifle bullets, and one leg hung crooked below the knee.

"Know 'em, do you?" Livingston asked. "Maybe you can send word to their papa. . . ."

"I buried his papa in Virginia," Willie said, eyeing Mills

44

with eyes grown steel-cold. Willie then bent down and pried a thin sheet of paper from Polk's fingers. After reading three neatly typed lines, Willie's insides turned to ice.

"What's that?" Livingston asked.

"Telegram," Willie said, offering it to the sheriff. "You never talked to these fellows at all. And you never saw this boy steal anything, Mills! They were on their way to a job in Young County. Rounding up cattle!"

"Who says?" Mills asked, quieting.

"The offer's spelled out clear, right here!" Willie exclaimed, as he waved the telegram in his hand. "He was going to tell you as much when you shot him. Look at these men! Men? This little one's not yet shaved. And they haven't a one of them drawn a gun!"

"Butchery," Joe muttered as he knelt beside the youngest. "I know this boy. He belongs to Albert Driscoll. Runs a tradin' post on the Little Wichita."

"He's right, Mr. Mills," one of the cowboys said, growing pale. "That's Davey Driscoll. He'd never—"

"Hold your tongue, Culpepper!" Mills shouted.

"Too bad," Livingston said, tearing the telegram from Willie's fingers and pocketing it. "Awful young, them boys. I wonder why they turned to rustling."

Mills regained his composure.

"You plan to take them home?" Mills asked Willie.

"You figure *that* to be my business?" Willie cried. "No, that's the job of the man that shot 'em, I'd say."

"Me, I say leave them here," Livingston suggested. "Be a warning to others."

"It would," Mills readily agreed.

"I'll see they're buried," Willie announced, as he felt his fingers touch his pistol grips. "Unless you object?"

"You got nothing else to waste your time with, go ahead," Mills said, grinning. "And before you go spreading any stories about, keep in mind you weren't here. We had the law on our side, and witnesses will say as much."

"And what will God say?" Willie asked, gazing overhead. "I guess maybe He saw, didn't He? And there's something else you ought to know. Young Polk here's got an uncle with a talent for raising a ruckus. Might be he'll take this personal."

"Ought to keep a tighter rein on his kin," Livingston declared. "You leave me to settle any trouble comes of this, Mr. Mills. It's what you're paying me for."

"And here I thought it was the county paid you," Willie muttered.

"One's more or less the same as the other," Mills boasted.

Willie stared at them coldly. Then Mills turned and rode away, followed by the others. Sheriff Livingston went last. He seemed a bit uneasy about turning his back to Wil Fletcher.

Once they had left, Joe fetched a spade from the wagon and began scratching out a grave in the rocky ground. Willie spelled him after a quarter hour, and by noon the grave was finished. Willie bundled each corpse in a blanket and set it in the trench beside a companion. Then Joe shoveled dirt over the lifeless bundles.

"No matter how many times I do this, I can never get used to it," Willie remarked bitterly.

"Nobody can," Joe declared. "So, what do we do now?"

Willie shrugged his shoulders and kicked the spade.

"What *can* we do?" he asked. "Hope this is the end of it, I guess. It won't be."

CHAPTER 6

A cloud of dread had settled over Willie as he rode back to Salt Fork Crossing. Now, as he silently hammered shingles into place, his thoughts were filled with silent faces—those motionless bodies, with their stone-cold eyes, buried beside the river. They put him in mind of other youngsters buried on smoke-haunted battlefields from Tennessee to Pennsylvania. And later, on the Kansas plains and the mountains of Wyoming Territory.

When Ellen and the children returned, he avoided the cheerful faces of the little ones.

"Uncle Wil, aren't you coming down?" Billy asked.

"Got work to do," Willie had answered.

"Then I'm coming up," Billy had answered.

The boy climbed up the side of the house and sat beside a barrel of nails, waiting for Willie to notice. But Billy's sparkling eyes froze Willie's insides.

You don't know, Willie silently told the youngster. Once the killing starts, it never ends quickly.

"You mad or something?" Billy asked after a time.

"Just busy," Willie muttered.

He was, in fact, busy right through supper. Joe Eagle had to pry him off the roof at dusk.

47

"It's not your fault," Ellen told him as he headed for his horse.

"What's not my fault?" he asked, avoiding her probing eyes.

"Those boys down at the river."

"Joe told you."

"He didn't have to," she said, sighing. "Abner Mills and his hands boasted of it. And of how you showed up when it was all over. One of the cowboys had a bit too much whiskey and spilled the truth. It wasn't much more than a massacre."

"Not the first one," Willie mumbled.

"No, we've known a few," she said, touching his shoulder. "Willie, you shouldn't take your phantoms elsewhere. You need people around."

"You don't know," he answered.

"I *do* know," she said, gripping his wrists. "Don't you think I've buried my share of children? Forgetting the sickness in Kansas? I was there when the Scarlets raided this valley!"

"It's not the same."

"It isn't?"

"Before, there was an enemy, somebody to strike back at. They did it so neat . . . and legal. But it's just as wrong."

"Tragic," she said, slipping her arms around his back and pulling him close. "There are courts to try such cases. Your brother James has powerful friends. Maybe he—"

"Jamie's a senator, not a judge," Willie told her. "And he's done me one favor more than I'm due already. Besides, what court would pay mind to me? I got there after it was over. The sheriff took the telegram."

"Joe could testify to it."

"Oh? They'll have less use for him than for me. I'm not sure an Indian can even testify in a Texas court."

"But that's not all that's troubling you."

"Polk Rucker was one of the dead ones, Ellie."

"Ray's youngest," she said, sighing. "You feel you let Ray down."

"It's more than that," Willie confessed. "I know Riley. He'll hear. And when he does, that fool Mills will think Hell itself's come to Throckmorton County."

"I don't recall Riley as a vengeful man."

"For a month after Ray fell, Riley'd set off at night alone. He never said anything, but when he came back he'd have some Yank soldier's cap, or boots, or carbine. It was like he had his own personal battle going. And Ray was cut down—fair, if there is such a thing."

"The war's been over fifteen years, Willie," Ellen pointed out. "You've changed. Don't you suppose Riley has, too?"

"I haven't changed all that much, Ellie," Willie said grimly. "If it was Billy we'd buried, Abner Mills would be dead this very minute."

"Revenge won't bring back the dead."

"No, there's nothing'll do that," Willie said somberly. "But there aren't many men who have seen what I have. And the only thing keeps us going is a sense of justice. That's why Riley will come."

"I hope you're wrong."

"So do I. Because it may be that Riley won't hold Mills to be the only one responsible. He could blame me, too."

"No."

"Yes," Willie assured her. "That's why it's best I stay away from you and the little ones till Riley happens along. Once we sort things out, I'll come back."

"Will you?"

"Unless I'm dead," he said, shuddering.

As Willie lay asleep that night on a hillside overlooking Salt Fork Crossing, nightmares plagued his dreams. He saw the one-sided fight at the river over and over. And he saw Riley Rucker gallop through Esperanza shooting down men, women, even children.

"An eye for an eye! A tooth for a tooth!" the demonic rancher screamed.

Joe finally woke Willie an hour shy of dawn.

"You gone too crazy," the Cheyenne said, pointing to the tattered remains of a blanket Willie gripped in both hands. "The ghosts o' them boys's found you. You better leave 'em to go their way, Major, or they'll hurry you to your death."

"Might be a blessing," Willie declared.

"No, you got folks need you," Joe argued. "And horses to gentle. Don't forgot you promised twenty saddle mounts to Travis Cobb for his trail crew."

"There's twenty ready now," Willie grumbled, as he discarded the shredded blanket. "But I haven't checked on them lately."

"No time like now," Joe announced. "Be light soon."

"Fry up some bacon while I fetch the eggs," Willie suggested. "We'll look over the horses on our way into town."

"Goin' to marshal awhile?"

"They still pay me, you know. Cash money."

"Sure they do," Joe said, laughing.

Following breakfast, Willie led Joe off to the box canyon where the horses were penned up. The two of them counted the three dozen mustangs that made up Willie's horse herd, then inspected the individual ponies.

"They seem gentle enough, Joe," Willie remarked, after riding a roan stallion that had been particularly stubborn about allowing a saddle on its back.

"None of 'em's run off," Joe noted. "Guess that's somethin'."

"Be an unusual horse to jump this fence or climb a canyon wall," Willie said, staring at the steep slopes. "Grass is thin, though. Best we move 'em back to the river."

"Tomorrow?"

"Now," Willie said, as he dismounted the roan. He then

slid aside the rails of the fence and waved the lead horses through the gap. They galloped along eagerly, and in no time the animals were grazing contentedly along the Salt Fork.

"You still goin' to town?" Joe asked, when Willie turned the big gray toward Esperanza.

"Sure," Willie answered. "Might be good if you came along, too. I'm less likely to get into trouble with company there."

"Yeah? Since when?" Joe asked.

"You only say that 'cause you've never seen me alone," Willie grumbled. "And right now I only have to think of that Mills fellow to get bloodred mad."

"You might *should* get mad at that one, Major. He wants some tendin'."

"He's apt to get it, too," Willie declared.

They arrived in Esperanza a little before noon. The town was nearly deserted. Except for the scurrying of the children at midday recess down at the school, there were few signs of life. Willie did manage to wave at Dewey Hamer as he passed the mercantile Rupe operated on Front Street.

Willie dismounted at the jail. After tying the gray to the hitching post, he motioned for Joe to do likewise. There were three horses tethered to a rail in front of the bank. Otherwise life seemed to have halted in Esperanza.

Willie's first surprise came when he entered his office. Thurman Livingston sat behind the desk, his muddy boots perched atop Willie's correspondence.

"I believe that's my desk," Willie said, glaring at the sheriff.

"Is it?" Livingston asked.

"Yes," Willie said, grabbing the toe of Livingston's right boot and pulling so that the sheriff landed with a thud on the hard wooden floor. Livingston made a motion for his pistol, but Willie's foot closed on the lawman's fingers first.

"Get off!" Livingston cried.

"Now, see there," Willie replied, staring grimly at the sheriff. "That's your problem, Livingston. You have no manners. A man comes into his office and finds you squatting on his desk. He asks you nicely to move, and you give him grief. Now, you might want to change your tone. Elsewise those fingers might come to have an accident."

"Let him up, Fletcher!" Abner Mills growled from the doorway. The cattleman was holding a Remington revolver. He lowered it, though, as Joe Eagle tapped his shoulder with a Colt.

"You maybe need a manners lesson, too, mister?" Joe asked.

"You two seem mighty eager to find trouble!" Mills barked. "You will find me eager to accommodate you."

"Don't push, Mills." Willie said, adding weight to his foot. "Just now I'd as soon shoot you as spit."

"You won't, though," Mills said, grinning. "I know your kind, Marshal. You need a reason to fight. You have to have proof before accusing somebody. You string a thing out until the worst has happened."

"Oh?" Willie asked, his eyes blazing.

"Now, take Thurm here and me," Mills continued. "We know there's rustling going on. We know who's behind it. So we ride out and have done with it."

"Won't those boys steal another cow," Livingston boasted.

"Makes you mad we done your job so easy, doesn't it?" Mills asked. "Well, don't let that trouble you for long. I own this county now, and Esperanza in particular. The marshal of this town won't be answering to Iowa shopkeepers and gray-haired grannies anymore. He'll do my bidding."

"Will he?" Willie asked.

"I've scheduled an election for next week, Fletcher. By that time I'll have my own people installed at the bank, the telegraph, the livery, maybe even Hamer's place. You'll find we've swapped preachers, by the way. New man'll be along in April. And I've sent to St. Louis for a teacher to replace that Trent woman."

"Figure to've bought a whole town, have you?" Willie cried, stepping away from Livingston and eyeballing Mills. "It's easy to do, hereabouts."

"You're finished here, Fletcher!" Livingston shouted, as he sprang to his feet.

"Got a week left, Sheriff," Willie said, flashing a hateful grin at the ex-ranger. "Now get out."

"He stays," Mills demanded. "This office is now assigned to the county. I've turned it over to Thurm."

"Out!" Willie shouted, and Livingston retreated two steps. "You're welcome to it, Mills, only I've got some things to pack up."

When Willie drew a Winchester down from the gun rack, Mills complained, "That's town property!"

"You find any receipt for it?" Willie asked. "Don't you go telling me what's what! You've not been here long enough to kick the dust off your boots. I put the floor in this place, and Joe and I brought the furniture in from Albany. You're welcome to keep the shell, but the insides are mine."

"Put a price to it," Livingston said, grinning. "He'll pay it. Won't you, Mr. Mills?"

"What's reasonable," Mills muttered.

"Double it," Livingston suggested. "I believe you're right, Fletcher. We did get off on the wrong foot. You don't back down. Man like that's good to know."

"Sometimes," Willie said, ignoring the sheriff's outstretched hand.

"I'd judge you owe Fletcher here two hundred dollars," Livingston announced. "That's more than fair, wouldn't you say?"

"A lot more," Mills complained.

"Oh, you might buy more than furniture," Livingston said, nodding smugly. "Two hundred might provide some understanding. Respect, even."

"That's not something money can buy," Willie growled.

"Oh, but it is," Mills argued as he handed Willie a handful of banknotes. "Always has before."

"You make me sick," Willie said, waving Joe outside and stepping out after him.

Rupert Hamer met them halfway to their horses.

"I guess you know about this election business," Hamer said, pulling Willie aside. "By tomorrow, I'll have enough votes lined up to keep you in office. The thought of buying a whole town! He has his share of gumption!"

"And how many votes'll you have next week?" Willie asked. "Next month? You figure to stay in business if Mills opens himself up a mercantile and cuts prices?"

"I don't forget easy," Hamer said, gazing sourly as Mills stepped out of the jail house door. "We can fight him," he insisted.

"I've been fighting somebody or something twenty years now," Willie complained. "That's enough fighting for ten lifetimes. I'm sick of it. Here, Mills, you can have this star," Willie added, unpinning the metal badge and throwing it at the cattleman. "It won't mean anything now. It's law gives it power."

"Wrong," Mills objected. "It's money!"

"You'll find out for yourself," Willie warned. "Soon, too. And what's coming your way I wouldn't wish on a skunk."

"And just what is that?" Mills asked.

"Wait and see," Willie said, as he mounted the gray. "And remember how easy it all seemed at the river."

CHAPTER 7

Willie waited at Rupe Hamer's store as a clock ticked off the afternoon hours a minute at a time. He refused to admit how naked he felt without that simple slice of metal on his shirt. It had been there only a few months, and yet . . .

"We could've fought 'em," Joe mumbled.

"What's the use?" Willie replied, as he stared across the dusty road to the school. "Anyway, it's Ellie who'll take it hard."

"People won't stand for it," Hamer grumbled.

"What people?" young Dewey asked. "Uncle Rupe, there's almost nobody left. Four, maybe five kids at the school, besides the Trents and those four Mills snipes. And the Liggett girls'll be moving on next week."

"Hard to believe a man can buy a whole town," Hamer said, frowning heavily. "Maybe we should all head for California. Seems to me this country's cursed."

"Can't blame the land," Willie argued. "It's as good a place as any I've known. Hot as the devil in summer and sure to freeze you come winter, but it gives you honest sweat. Not much good for farming, but it raises good cows. And hardy horses."

"Speaking of which, you promised I could help work your stock," Dewey declared.

"Mostly they're ready to deliver," Willie explained.

"Good!" Dewey exclaimed. "Then you can take me mustanging instead."

"Not many wild horses to be found hereabouts anymore," Willie said, sighing.

"Not many," Joe agreed. "But some."

"What?" Willie asked.

"Saw 'em from Blood Mesa," the Cheyenne added. "Big black stallion and a fine harem. Take top hands to run 'em down, but then what'd we be, eh, Major?"

"And I'm coming along," Dewey announced.

"Don't you have a job here?" Willie asked.

"Uncle Rupe?" Dewey asked hopefully.

"He'd be no use to me, what with wild horses flooding his head every second," Hamer answered. "Better take him along with you, Wil. Only try not to drop him off any bluffs or break too many of his bones."

"That'd be up to the ponies," Willie said, giving Joe a nod.

With talk of mustanging filling the air, the time passed much more quickly. Finally Ellen rang the dismissal bell, and the handful of farm urchins spilled out the door. Alice Mills led her brothers along a minute later, and Ellen emerged with her four afterward.

"Where's your badge, Uncle Wil?" Billy blurted when Willie walked over to where the wagon waited.

"Willie?" Ellen asked.

"Seems Mr. Mills has somebody else in mind," Willie told them.

"I shouldn't be surprised," Ellen said, handing over a brief letter of dismissal. "Seems the books were only the beginning. Well, after next week I wouldn't have much of a class anyway. He enclosed two hundred dollars."

"Nice of him," Willie said, turning to where Abner Mills stood beside his children.

"It's not worth fighting over," Ellen said, firmly gripping Willie's hand. "And I was growing tired of the job."

Willie didn't believe a word of it, but he swallowed his arguments and hurried to help Billy harness the team.

"Have you heard the news?" Dewey called to the youngsters, as he brought a saddled pinto over from a corral behind the livery. "We're going mustangin'!"

"We?" Billy asked.

"You're going to school," Willie told the boy. "Joe and I're huntin' horses. Once we deliver the string we owe your Uncle Trav."

"And I'm comin' along," Dewey pointed out.

"If you can quit jabbering long enough," Willie muttered. "Be three, four days getting the horses down to Clear Fork, and another readying ourselves for the hunt, Dewey."

"And there's still the roof to finish," Ellen said, as she helped Anne up onto the wagon seat.

"I can do that," Dewey volunteered. "And more besides."

"Joe?" Willie asked.

"That white boy'll likely get in the way more'n help," Joe growled, "but best you bring him along, Major. He hammers good, and he don't eat too much."

"Only his weight once a week," Billy complained. "Remember when he was with us last year?"

"I brought in my share of meat, didn't I, Wil?" Dewey asked. "I'm close to seventeen now, too. Mostly a man."

"Sure you are, Dewey," Ellen said, giving the young man a pat on his bony shoulder. "Now hurry and hitch up those horses, William Trent. Elsewise we'll be eating supper by moonlight."

"Can't have that now," Willie declared, lending a hand. In short order the horses were hitched, the children loaded, and the wagon was rolling homeward.

*   *   *

The three days that followed were a blur. As promised, Dewey finished shingling the roof, while Willie and Joe delivered twenty saddle horses to Travis Cobb's ranch on the Clear Fork of the Brazos.

"Fine animals, as usual," Travis said as he settled the account. "So, are you coming north with us this spring?"

"Maybe," Willie said, shifting his weight nervously. "Might have need of work."

"I noticed somethin' missin'," Travis said, glancing at the empty spot on Willie's vest. "We're not so far away that we don't hear things. Why don't you sell out and swing on down here? There's a nice stretch east of us that would make a fine horse ranch. Be nice havin' Ellen close by, too. The children would have cousins to get into mischief."

"I got horses to chase down just now," Willie explained.

"And next year? You're the one told me a man's got to change with the times, remember? There's a railroad marchin' west from Fort Worth. Due in Weatherford soon, and from there it'll march all the way to California. Won't be many years of trail drivin' left. That'll cut into the horse trade considerable."

"Always be a market for horses in Texas," Willie argued.

"But not for range ponies. Be the breeders make a livin' of it."

"I got it in my mind to be one of 'em, too."

"Man won't need to be in the wilds to breed good stock," Travis said, gazing intently at his old friend. "And you'd have steady buyers down here."

"I appreciate that, too," Willie replied. "And I'll give long thought to it."

"Do that, Willie. And put some distance between you and this Mills jasper. He's got less than a stalwart reputation down Laredo way. It's said he hung the sons of two Mexican dons. They swore to even the score, so he hightailed it north."

"Seems good at fighting youngsters," Willie said, grinding his teeth.

"I heard about that, too," Travis added. "Watch yourself. Throckmorton County could have visitors."

Willie nodded, then turned to leave. By nightfall he was back at Coon Hollow, making the final preparations for the mustang hunt.

Always before, Willie had welcomed the opportunity to test himself against the unbridled defiance of wild horses. It was much more than the opportunity to convert long hours of toil into cash at market.

"It's a challenge," Dewey declared, as they rode past Blood Mesa.

"More'n that," Joe said solemnly.

"Then what?" Dewey asked.

"No words for it," Joe answered. "Major?"

"It's a thing of the spirit," Willie declared. "You can have kinship with any horse, but one that's never known the open places, the wild ways, well, it just never gives you the same ride."

"You don't break horses like I see others do."

"A whip never brought out a pony's best effort," Willie observed.

"He does it the old way," Joe noted. "As I'd do."

"Cheyennes knew," Willie said, nodding to Joe. "Me, I learned it from the Comanches. You can rope a wild thing, even saddle it, but there's a part that always stays wild. Or dies. Smart man uses the wildness for the speed it gives him."

"But you got to stay atop him," Dewey said, tilting his hat forward so he could scratch his head. "It seems to me you got to bend him to your will."

"Or convince him to cooperate," Willie explained. "You'll see how it's done. First, though, we've got to catch up with those ponies. And rope 'em."

"Best thing to do's run 'em into that box canyon," Joe

declared. "Fence is still there. All we got to do's slide the rails into place, and we got 'em."

"All right, Joe. But how do we turn that black demon into the trap?" Willie asked.

"That's for you to figure, Major," Joe answered, grinning. "You got the smarts, remember?"

Dewey laughed, and Joe slapped his horse into a gallop so as to avoid Willie's reply. The three horsemen chased each other across hills and ravines for close to three miles before Joe picked up the herd's trail.

"This way," Joe called, waving to his companions.

They galloped a quarter mile before halting. Just below, not far from the cave where Willie had brought Ellen and the little ones, fifty mustangs grazed, unaware of their visitors.

"There's the black on the left," Willie said, swallowing hard. The animal's powerful shoulders and proud head marked him as a rare beast—the offspring of a thoroughbred likely run off some ranch during the heyday of Comanche horse-stealing. For a time Willie was transfixed by the animal. He could hardly breathe.

"How do we do it?" Joe finally whispered.

"Head 'em toward the box," Willie explained. "Take the left, Joe. I'll run the black myself. Who knows? I might even get a rope on him. If not, turn the mares and colts toward the corral."

"And me?" Dewey asked.

"Bring up the rear, Dewey. Scream to high heaven. And try to keep 'em from breaking off to the right. Understand?"

"Yes," Dewey replied. "I'll do my best, Wil."

"Never considered otherwise," Willie responded, giving the young man a slap on the shoulder. "Best we get about it."

Joe set off first to encircle the left. Then Willie gave a whoop and charged the black. Behind him Dewey shouted and galloped along. In seconds the horses were stampeding west—toward the box canyon trap.

Willie raced his gray alongside the powerful black stallion and readied a rope, but the wild devil would not be caught. It raced on the wind, and the closest Willie came was ten feet or so.

Once the big black flashed a backward glance, as if to show its disdain. Then, lathered but barely showing any signs of faltering, it broke to the right, eluded Willie's rope, and charged past Dewey Hamer. Some of the mares followed, but Willie managed to cut the others off. Even though the stallion had escaped, the mustangers still drove twenty-three horses into the box canyon and slid the rails across the gate, sealing their escape route.

"He's a devil, that black," Joe observed afterward.

"Just showed us who's king of this range," Willie said, laughing. "The game's far from over, though."

Dewey and Joe seemed less convinced.

That night the three horse-hunters made camp below Blood Mesa. In the distance the big black raced back and forth, gathering what remained of its harem and snorting its defiance under a full moon.

"Was a time I was that free," Willie remarked. "Back when I was fourteen. I took off from the ranch and lived on my own with old Yellow Shirt's Comanches."

"I heard o' him," Joe said. "Was a fierce fighter. Had the Mexicans plenty scairt. Cheyennes, too."

"Fought Papa for years. Then, after two of Yellow Shirt's sons were killed, he had a vision. Made peace," Willie said, recalling the day he'd sat at his father's side near the tall oak where the two leaders had smoked the pipe. "Yellow Shirt never again killed a white man. Was riding out to argue peace the night some German farm boy shot him dead. Wasn't much peace after that."

"He the one taught you to work horses?" Dewey asked.

"And much more besides," Willie explained. "He knew things, that old man. Saw the future. He tried to tell me what war was, but I was fifteen. Can't explain battle to a youngster with no ear for cautious words."

"Ain't in the way o' things," Joe agreed.

"So I suppose I envy you, boy," Willie called to the black. "You can still taste the freedom of the open range."

Willie knew it wouldn't last. Elsewhere they were already stringing up fences. And the railroad was coming.

His thoughts were broken by the sound of a twig snapping twenty feet away. Willie jumped to his feet and reached for his pistol, but a voice froze his movements.

"No need o' that, Major," Riley Rucker called, as he stepped into the light. Beside him were a dozen men, each holding a rifle at the ready. "Just came for a chat's, all."

"Strange way to go about it," Willie said, eyeing them nervously. "Most folks call by daylight."

"Wasn't sure of my welcome," Riley explained as he approached. "Warren, this the man you met with?"

"The first time," Warren answered, as he joined his uncle. "Told us to clear out, but he didn't shoot bullets at us."

"The youngsters helped themselves to one of my steers," Willie said, recounting the episode. "Care for some coffee, Riley?"

"Came for conversation," Riley replied. "Now, Warren, you butchered a range steer, did you? Not the smartest thing to do nowadays. But no reason to kill a man, either."

"I didn't kill anyone," Willie insisted.

"Somebody did," Warren said angrily. "Polk and I headed north after you warned us to skedaddle. But we come to get a telegram promisin' work. Was half a dozen of us took off with a wagon, bound south. We camped on Salt Fork—on your land, to hear folks tell it. I was off huntin' fresh meat. Come back to the sound o' shootin'. My brother was dead. The rest, too. And I saw you and that Indian there buryin' 'em."

"Didn't do the shooting, though," Willie said.

"But you'd know who did," Riley growled. "Eh, Major?"

"I don't suppose you'd be asking so as to swear out a warrant for their arrest?" Willie asked, frowning.

"You know me, Major. I settle accounts," Riley said, sliding his fingers along the barrel of his Winchester. "Who was it?"

"And if I won't tell you?" Willie asked.

"Didn't figure you would," Riley muttered. He then sat down and handed his rifle to Warren. "Those boys are all that's left of Ray, you know. You was there when he fell, and you know I promised to look after 'em. Was only so much I could do. Now Polk's dead, and there's a price to be paid for that."

"It's said in Esperanza we was rustlin' stock," Warren spoke, as he balled his fists and pounded the ground. "We were headed for work. Polk tried to tell 'em."

"You heard him?" Willie asked.

"No, but there were others there. Fellow named Culpepper had a fit of conscience," Warren explained. "Paid Dave Driscoll's folks a call. Polk didn't get half a dozen words out 'fore they took to shootin'. Wasn't a single bullet fired in return."

"You buried them boys," Riley said bitterly. "They was shot to pieces, wasn't they? Well?"

"You know how it is in a fight," Willie said, struggling to hold back his own rage. "People get excited."

"They was just boys!" Riley shouted. "What manner o' animal can this Mills fellow be?"

"You know who did it, then," Willie said, sighing.

"I only come by as a courtesy to hear your tellin'," Riley explained. "Warren had in mind you played a part, but he don't know you. You'd be death on horseback if you had good reason, but you'd never shoot down boys camped on a river. No man changes that much."

"So what are your plans, Riley?" Willie asked.

The man's answering gaze chilled Willie to the bone.

"There's courts," Willie suggested. "Laws."

"Been days already," Riley answered. "Shoot, I was in

town to visit this Livingston fellow. Calls himself a sheriff, but I remember him for a hired killer up Tascosa way. Good as said Polk was a cow thief. So I'd say we got a couple o' folks to settle with.''

"Riley, Mills has a lot of men," Willie warned.

"And I got lots o' friends," Riley answered. "Do yourself a favor, Major. Stay clear o' Esperanza for a time."

"It isn't the town's fault," Willie argued.

"I know who's to blame," Riley barked. "And that's who'll pay. Sorry I interrupted your evenin'. Be goin' now."

And with that said, Riley Rucker waved his companions back into the shadows. The darkness swallowed them, and the sound of departing horses marked the end of the meeting.

CHAPTER 8

Willie tossed and turned in his sleep that night. He couldn't erase Riley Rucker's vengeful gaze from his mind, and a hundred nightmares bedeviled him.

Willie finally awoke as dawn spread a burnt orange glow across the horizon. The chill night and a heavy dew had left him cold and stiff. He felt like a kinked rope. Only by rubbing the soreness out of his legs and twisting his neck in all directions was he able to stand. Nearby, Dewey Hamer and Joe Eagle lay sprawled on blankets in their makeshift camp beside the box canyon corral.

Willie was tempted to rouse them, but the disheveled state of Dewey's bedding testified to a restless night. As to Joe, well, he would awaken as the sun climbed into the sky. A few months of civilization had yet to overpower Joe Eagle's Cheyenne upbringing.

As Willie set about tying twists of prairie grass into kindling, he half forgot about Rucker's visit. Perhaps, he thought, it was only a bad dream. But there were too many fresh horse tracks—left by shod horses. Willie judged Riley had brought ten men, maybe more. A small army had come to Throckmorton County.

"That fool Mills," Willie muttered. The rancher was certain to face hard times now. And though Mills was shrewd in his way, cleverly manipulating people, politicians, elections, and the sort, it was a deadlier game he would soon be playing.

"How will you do it, Riley?" Willie asked the whining wind.

A terrible thought then haunted Willie. An eye for an eye? It wouldn't be Mills Riley'd go after. No, a boy had died. A boy would pay.

Lord, if he's been to town he knows about those kids at the school, Willie realized. Ellen and the little ones will be there. And she, of course, would never surrender one of her charges to armed intruders.

"Joe!" Willie shouted, as he ran toward where his saddle rested. "Get up!"

Joe leaped to his feet, shook himself awake, and stared in wonder as Willie hurriedly saddled his horse.

"Major, you crazed?" the Cheyenne asked.

"No, but Riley Rucker just might be," Willie explained. "He's apt to go after the school in Esperanza. What a fool I am for not thinking of it last night!"

"Be two hours 'fore we can get to town," Joe said, as he threw on his clothes and began saddling his pinto.

"If we hurry and ride cross-country, we can cut twenty minutes off."

"And lame a horse," Joe complained.

"It's Ellie!" Willie exclaimed.

"What's all the ruckus?" Dewey cried, moaning as he sat up.

"Nothing," Willie grumbled as he checked his cinch.

"Major figures those fellows from last night might pay a call on Esperanza," Joe explained. "To the school."

"Best I get dressed then," Dewey said, throwing off his blankets.

"Be hard riding and maybe harder fighting," Willie de-

66

clared. "I'd as soon you stayed and watched the horses, Dewey."

"There you go, leavin' me behind again," the young man said, shaking his head as he pulled on his boots. "Told you I'm sixteen. And I wasn't altogether unwelcome when you took on those Scarlets."

"You had reason then," Willie said, climbing atop the gray. "You're not needed for this business."

"I might come in handy just the same," Dewey argued, as he dragged his saddle to where his pinto was picketed. "You try to sneak into that school, somebody's sure to take notice. Me now, I might pass for a pupil. Huh?"

"Boy's got a point," Joe admitted, as he mounted his horse. "Only be a minute wasted waitin'."

Willie frowned, but he didn't ride off. Instead he waited for Dewey to saddle up and get mounted. When the boy nodded he was ready Willie nudged the gray toward town, then urged the animal into a gallop.

They rode with abandon across the broken country, splashing through icy streams and leaping narrow ravines. Only where the washes were wide and deep did Willie slow the pace. Even then he hurried the gray down the steep embankments and then up the opposite slope. A sense of dread was settling over him, and each moment a fresh specter added its torments.

They arrived in Esperanza early—but not early enough. Just glancing down Front Street Willie could count a dozen extra horses tied here and there. Mostly the animals were in pairs so as not to attract attention. Willie had a marshal's eye, though, even if he lacked a badge. Clearly there were visitors about.

It was Joe who took note of the brands.

"That's the fifth 'Lazy R' already," the Cheyenne pointed out.

"An R, huh?" Willie noted, marking a shadow outside the bank in his memory. "I'd guess it for Rucker's outfit."

"Headin' for the school?" Joe asked, as Willie dismounted.

"For Rupe Hamer's place," Willie answered. "Give me your horse, Dewey. I'll tie 'em both off."

"And I'll have a look inside the school," Dewey added.

"You take some care," Willie warned. "And make sure you mention your name. Don't want you being mistaken for a Mills."

"Worried over me?" Dewey asked, grinning.

"There's cause," Willie declared. "Be careful."

"I will be," Dewey pledged, as he headed across the street toward the school.

"Joe, ride on down Front Street and eyeball the place," Willie suggested. "Then come back to Hamer's store."

"Easy to do," Joe replied, giving his pinto a gentle tap on the rump. "Come on, boy. Not much more ridin' this day."

Willie then saw to the horses and stepped inside Hamer's store. There was a youngish stranger in there, a red-haired cowboy with watery green eyes.

"How are you, Major?" Hamer asked from behind his counter. "Found those horses yet?"

"Ran twenty or so into a canyon," Willie answered, ignoring the clear anxiety of the storekeeper. "Be a good season's work gentling them. Glad young Dewey came along. I can use the help."

"You raise horses, do you?" the stranger asked.

"Try to," Willie said, smiling. "Name's Fletcher. Wil Fletcher. You in need of a mount, Mr. . . ."

"Tolly Compton," the cowboy answered. "Always lookin' for a good saddle pony. Thought once I might breed horses myself."

"It's a fine way to go broke, I suppose, but you never tire of the days. Ponies always got a few surprises in store for you."

"They do have their ways," Compton agreed.

"You ride with this Lazy R outfit?" Willie slipped in.

"What's that?" Compton said, tensing.

"Was wondering if you might be with the Lazy R's. I noticed a lot of horses in town today with that brand. Can't seem to place it."

"I rode for Lazy R last summer, and the boss gave me leave to keep my horse," Compton explained. "Run across some others from the outfit north o' here. We thought to head down to Clear Fork and hunt up a trail herd to drive to Kansas."

"There are some good outfits down there," Willie admitted. "Nobody raising horses thereabouts, but—"

Willie swallowed the words as gunshots erupted down Front Street.

"Easy there," Compton cautioned, as he revealed a drawn Colt revolver. "Now you just join Mr. Hamer back of this counter."

"Don't think I will," Willie answered, diving out the door, then drawing his own Colt and firing a shot in Compton's direction. The startled cowboy hadn't bothered to cock his hammer, and now he only managed to fumble the gun onto the floor.

"Get out!" Willie hollered, as he stepped inside. Compton abandoned his gun and ran out into the street.

"You should've shot him!" Hamer exclaimed excitedly. "They're robbing the bank."

"That one's not," Willie argued. "Anyway, I don't plan on starting any personal feud with those boys. Anybody at the school?"

"Two men," Hamer said, cracking open a shotgun and inserting two shells. "I saw Dewey head that way."

"He's been in there a bit now," Willie observed. "I believe I'll take a look."

Hamer nodded. Joe Eagle galloped back up Front Street, shook off a shudder, and dismounted.

"There's folks all over the place up that way," Joe said, shaking his head. "A pair of 'em shot bullets at me. They're most interested in the bank, but I noticed one of 'em's cut the telegraph wires."

"That would make sense," Willie said, nodding.

"They seem to be waitin' for somethin'," Joe claimed.

"Not something," Willie declared. "Someone. Abner Mills."

But it was equally possible the raiders already had what they wanted—in the school. It was that notion that spurred Willie to action. He raced across the street, then cautiously approached the school. He got within ten feet of the place when Warren Rucker appeared in the door, pistol in hand, holding Cobb Trent as a shield.

"Uncle Wil!" the boy shouted.

"You're a hair late for the party, Major," Warren called. "But I guess you figured things out just the same."

"You've got no business with that boy," Willie said, swallowing hard as he stepped toward the door. "He's done nothing to hurt you or yours."

"That right, teacher lady?" Warren asked, as he glanced inside the school. "You sure you ain't a Mills, boy?"

"Mama said not to say," Cobb replied.

Willie frowned. He'd been slow to catch on, as usual. Ellen wasn't telling the Ruckers who the children were. In that way the Mills youngsters were protected. For the moment, at least.

"That's close enough," Warren announced, when Willie reached the wooden steps leading to the door. "Hate to shoot you, Major. Not now I know who you are. Papa left some letters. Your name came up a time or two."

"Your father was a friend," Willie explained. "Polk's dying as he did hit me hard."

"Then you understand what we're about, don't you?" the young man asked.

"Your business is with Mills, not these kids," Willie argued. "They've not hurt anybody."

"They kilt my brother!" Warren shouted excitedly. "Killin' the old man wouldn't hurt him much. Shoot, he'd be cold straight away, and that'd be that. Uncle Riley come up with a neat little plan, though. We hear Mills'

70

got three boys and a girl. Four of 'em! We kill 'em off slow, one at a time. He's got plenty o' time to suffer that way.''

"You can't," Willie objected.

"And who's to stop us?"

"I am," Willie said, gazing hard at the young man's moist eyes. "I got no love for Mills myself, but murdering children's past reason."

"We won't kill 'em all, Major. Just the Mills kids," Warren promised.

Willie made a half turn away from the door. Then, quick as lightning, he turned and leaped up the stairs. Warren got off a single shot, but Cobb managed to jolt the young cowboy's arm at the last second and the shot went wide. Willie, meanwhile, landed atop Warren and pinned the young man to the floor. It was a simple matter then to pry the pistol from his fingers.

"Cobb, you see Joe over there?" Willie whispered, as Joe dragged a hay cart up Front Street. The boy nodded. "Run over and give him a hand, won't you?"

"But Mama—"

"Go!" Willie said, giving the youngster a nudge. Cobb raced over to the hay cart. Willie meanwhile got Warren to his feet and pointed the way inside the school.

"Warren!" Riley shouted from back of Ellen's desk. "What was all that noise about?"

"We had a disagreement of sorts," Willie explained, as he followed, pistol in hand.

"I didn't have much luck," Dewey said, staring up from the floor. Young Hamer's lip was bloody, and his left eye was closed.

"You don't aim to mix in my business, do you, Major?" Riley asked. "We soldiered together, true, and that'd make us friends by ordinary accounts. But this is personal. I got an account to settle."

"You won't settle it terrifying them," Willie said, pointing to the assembled children. "I've got a personal interest

71

here, too. That littlest girl there, and the boys on the left there. They go right now.''

"Do they?'' Riley asked, cradling a shotgun.

"They go, or I unload a pistol into Warren here,'' Willie said grimly.

"Do that and I'll kill you.''

"You might try,'' Willie answered. "But you know better'n most I'm no easy man to kill.''

"Likewise,'' Riley growled.

"Billy, Ellis, take your sister outside and find Joe,'' Willie instructed. "Ellen, see if you can help Dewey along.''

"Major!'' Riley shouted.

"He's bound to know which o' the ones that're left is a Mills and which ain't,'' Warren said, gathering his wits.

"He'll never tell, though,'' Riley grumbled. "That right, Major?''

"It's a poor kind of revenge, Riley,'' Willie declared, as he lowered his pistol. "Look at them. Six poor children you've got scared out of their britches.''

"That girl there's as big as Polk was,'' Warren argued.

"Sure,'' Willie admitted. "And that one boy's almost big enough to shave. Make you a tall man, Warren, shooting such folks!''

"You know it's their father I want,'' Riley said, turning toward the window and peering out onto Front Street. "I want to peel him like an apple, hear him scream. I want him to hurt the way I do, standin' here and thinkin' about poor Polk lyin' in that heartless hole you dug for him at Salt Fork.''

"Tell me, Riley, when you killed those Yanks back in Virginia, did it ease the loss you felt any?'' Riley frowned, and Willie nodded. "It sure didn't bring Ray back to us. It's a fool's errand you've come on. In the end it'll get you killed. Warren, too. Maybe those other boys out yonder.''

"So you'd have me walk away and do nothin'?''

72

"See a judge."

"I know men like Mills," Riley said, grinding his teeth. "They buy and sell judges like stud horses. I want justice for Polk, I'll have to bring it about myself."

"By shooting children?"

"However."

"Riley, you say you always settle accounts."

"I do."

"Then I'm handing you a bill of sorts. I buried Polk and those others. I figure that entitles me to something. And there was that time you got taken by that Yank patrol on the Rapidan. I went in myself and brought you out. Remember?"

"So I owe you. Not denyin' it."

"I'm asking payment," Willie said, stepping over to the cowering youngsters.

"Name it," Riley muttered, as he dipped a hand into his side pocket. "I've done well since the war."

"It's not dollars I want," Willie said, stiffening. "It's these six here."

"Don't do it, Uncle Riley," Warren pleaded.

"It's done," Riley said, waving them toward the door. "Hey, you there," he added, reaching out and snatching Jacob Mills by the ear. "See, I knew as soon as the other boys left that the three left would be Mills spawn. I'll abide by your bargain, though, Major."

Riley then gazed hard into the eleven-year-old's eyes and tore open the boy's shirt.

"I could just as soon've ripped your heart out," Riley added. "Tell that to your pa when you come across him. And tell him I'll be back."

"That wasn't called for," Willie complained, as Jake raced past, bound for the door.

"Was a time I took orders from you, Willie Delamer," Riley said, pacing beside Ellen's desk. "No more. Any debt I owed is paid in full now. As to this town, well, it's a different sort of debt I owe it. You care for that gal and her

73

brood, keep 'em away from Esperanza. You value your own skin, keep it clear, too.''

Riley Rucker then stormed out onto Front Street, directed a final taunt at the Mills youngsters, collected his men, and left town.

CHAPTER 9

Willie stumbled to the door of the school, his mind a jumble of confusion.

"Willie?" Ellen called, leaving the children with Joe Eagle and rushing over. "Are you all right?"

"Sure," Willie muttered.

"I never was so glad to see anybody in all my life," she declared, hugging him tightly.

"You saved us," Billy added, as he ran over. "I got to tell you, I was plenty scared."

"It's your mama was the brave one," Willie insisted. "Stood her ground, didn't give an inch."

"I didn't have much choice," Ellen replied. "Those children were my responsibility. You, on the other hand . . ."

"Had a gun," Willie argued. "Was pretty stupid of me to send the boys off. Never thought it'd give away Mills' boys."

"You were only thinking of Billy and Ellis," she said, holding him tighter. "No one could blame you for that."

"I'd've blamed myself if Riley'd done those kids any harm."

"He didn't, and I'd judge that to be your doing, too."

"Old debts," Willie mumbled.

"Papa!" Alice Mills yelled then, and Willie stepped out into the street to watch the cattleman's arrival. To Willie's surprise, Abner Mills wasn't riding in off the range. No, Mills was walking out of the bank office, ambling along as if nothing had happened.

"He was here the whole time," Dewey grumbled.

"Doesn't seem possible," Willie said, sighing.

But soon enough he was proven wrong, for Mills and Thurman Livingston had witnessed everything.

"Brave thing you did, Fletcher," Mills noted, as he wrapped an arm around Alice and continued on to where Albert was trying to comfort a tearful Jacob. Little Jonathan stood beside the Trent boys, solemn-faced and silent.

"Told you it was a mistake to send him packing," Livingston declared, as he joined the gathering. "I've seen you before, haven't I? In the Cimarron country, maybe."

"Maybe," Willie confessed. "I don't remember, though."

"It was a few years back," Livingston said, shaking his head. "I wasn't much to remember then."

Nor now, Willie thought.

"I never seen the like, Pa," Albert said, turning toward Willie. "Those fellows charged inside the school with murder in their eyes. Ordered Miz Trent to turn us over or they'd kill everyone. She just crossed her arms and told 'em to go to blazes."

"The younger one looked us over," Alice added. "Turned the room upside down. Looked in our coats, searched high and low for clues."

"Good thing we didn't have our names on anything," Albert declared. "I believe they would have shot us dead."

"Might have, anyway," Alice said. "Only, Dewey there rushed in, saying he had a message for Miz Trent. The old one got into a tangle with Dewey and beat him some. Were shots outside, and the young one took Cobb outside.''

"That's when Marshal Fletcher came," Albert announced. "He knew those men. I didn't get everything, and I was mighty worried when Billy and Ellis left. But the older one . . .''

"The mean one," Alice added.

"He owed the marshal something," Albert went on. "So they let us go.''

"But he said he'd come back!" Jake shouted, staring wild-eyed at his father. "Pa, he tore my shirt and said next time it'd be my heart!''

"There's no sense to this," Livingston said, scratching his ear. "I know some o' those boys. Regular cowboys, and nothin' more. What's raised their dander?''

"Recognize the leader, Thurm?" Mills asked.

"Know the brand," the sheriff answered. "Lazy R. That's the Rucker outfit.''

"I've had no dealings with them," Mills insisted.

"Yes you have," Willie said sourly. "You recall I warned you trouble would come of that business at the river.''

"Kin?" Livingston asked.

"The worst kind," Willie answered. "Riley Rucker. He figures you murdered his nephew. By all accounts, I'd say he was right.''

"You weren't there," Mills growled. "And neither was he. He can't know it was me.''

"Why not?" Willie asked. "Your hands have jabbered about that day across half of Texas.''

"And you know this Rucker?" Mills asked.

"We served together in the war," Willie explained. "He's got a particular sense of justice, and he won't be put off. He *will* be back.''

"This Rucker's a bad sort to cross," Livingston added. "I heard how a thief stole one of his horses. Rucker chased him clear to Arizona Territory. Shot him dead.''

"Stories," Mills said, laughing. "If he'd had in mind to do something, he would have."

"He did, Pa," Jake cried, showing his tattered shirt.

"You've got other shirts, son," Mills told the boy. "He could have robbed the bank, but he didn't. Like as not he's not even certain what happened down at the river."

"He doesn't have to be," Willie said, frowning. "But you believe what you will, Mills. It's your business."

"Not entirely," Mills objected. "You've done me a service, Fletcher. A big one. I'd like to offer you a reward. Say, a hundred dollars?"

"Keep your money," Willie suggested. "Whatever I did wasn't for you. If Riley Rucker came back and put a bullet through your fool head, I'd find no fault with him for it. Was for Ellen and the little ones I did what I did. You see, Mills, I'd argue against shooting any youngster, even one of yours."

"Maybe you'd like your job back as town marshal?" Mills asked. "And of course, we'll insist Mrs. Trent stay on at the school. Our children couldn't be in better hands."

"I wouldn't dignify such an offer with an answer," Ellen answered.

"You keep the star," Willie added. "As for those youngsters, I'd keep them close to home for a time. Seems Riley's bound and determined to even the score through them."

"Thurm, send for a couple of good men," Mills ordered. "You're certain you won't sign on yourself, Fletcher?"

"I got horses to work," Willie said, turning toward the store, where his horse anxiously pawed the dust.

"I'd pay top wages!" Mills shouted.

"Then maybe you can buy Riley off," Willie said, untying the gray. "You said money'd buy anything, didn't you?"

"It will, too," Mills declared.

"Not everything," Willie muttered.

He then watched over the scene, while Billy and Cobb got the team hitched to the wagon. Ellen, meanwhile, collected some books and papers from the school and closed the door.

"I left some things for your St. Louis teacher," she told Mills. "I wish him luck."

"Won't you reconsider?" Mills asked.

"No reason to," Willie said. The little ones piled into the wagon, while Ellen climbed atop the seat. Then she poked the team into motion.

"Coming, Joe?" Willie called. "Dewey?"

"We got horses to work, don't we?" Joe answered, as he mounted his pony. Dewey came along as well.

They headed out toward Salt Fork Crossing, but only a mile outside town Willie's attention was drawn by a thick column of black smoke.

"Uncle Wil?" Billy asked in alarm.

"The Gunnerson place," Dewey said, frowning. "Or what used to be it."

"Mills was usin' it for a line camp," Joe added.

"Riley isn't wasting any time, is he?" Willie asked.

Ellen turned the wagon in that direction, but Willie argued against it.

"Not our business," he claimed. "Who cares if they burn half the farms in Throckmorton County? We've got our own worries."

"There could be folks hurt out there," Ellen said, stubbornly refusing to alter her course.

"Three cowboys and a cook, last time I rode by," Joe explained. "I saw the cook that day at the river, Major. Can't be sure about the others."

"It won't much matter to Riley," Willie said, urging the gray into a gallop. Joe was instantly at his side, and Dewey trailed along as best he could.

The three of them beat the wagon to the scene by ten minutes, and Willie was glad. The house, barn, and outbuildings were still blazing, but it was all over for the occupants. The cook lay sprawled beside the well, two holes in his chest and one arm near torn off by a shotgun blast.

The other three were bunched behind a woodpile.

"Looks like they put up a fight," Dewey noted, pointing to the rifles frozen in their lifeless hands.

"Not much o' one," Joe declared. "Was over quick enough."

"That's Blake Lindsay there," Dewey said, as he slid off his saddle and stood beside the body of a young man in his late teens. "He used to pick up supplies at Uncle Rupe's store. He wasn't much of a hand. I could throw a rope better."

"Well, he's done all the roping he'll ever do," Willie judged.

"Still figure it's none of our business?" Dewey asked.

"Hope to heaven it's not," Willie replied. "This is just the beginning. Just Riley's calling card."

"What?" Dewey cried.

"Putting Mills on notice. Be going after the other camps, then the main ranch," Willie explained.

"This'll put a scare in his hands," Joe added. "Even up the numbers some."

"There's four men dead here!" Dewey exclaimed.

"Were four at the river, too," Willie pointed out. "More, before it's finished."

Willie managed to drag the bodies clear of the woodpile before Ellen arrived with the wagon. His one regret was that he didn't have a blanket to cover the bodies with. Ellen, who had seen worse during her turbulent years in Kansas, merely grew pale and silent. The children huddled together in terror.

"You'll want the wagon," Ellen finally announced, as she helped Anne to the ground. "We can ride home with Joe."

"What would I want the wagon for?" Willie asked.

"To take them to town," Ellen explained. "It's a small

comfort to be buried in the churchyard, I know, but it's easily done. And you'll have a chance to confer with Sheriff Livingston.''

''What for?'' Willie asked. ''It's clear what's happened. Mills will be along once he sees the smoke.''

''They're our neighbors, Willie,'' she argued. ''I deem it a duty.''

''They'd hardly return the favor,'' Willie complained. ''Who came to help us in our time of need? Was Abner Mills up on the roof nailing shingles? Nobody but Dewey and his uncle even bothered to pass the time of day. I'd guess I've done Mills enough favors this day.''

''You can't hide from this sort of trouble, Willie,'' Ellen insisted.

''No? Would you ride into the middle of it? Only death's waiting down that trail. Trust me to know. I've been there often enough.''

''You can't pretend we're not involved!''

''No, but do we have to jump in over our heads, Ellie? It won't be lost on Riley, you know. I've upset his plans once. It'd be a bad habit to start doing it regular.''

''Please?'' she begged.

''I'll take 'em back,'' Dewey volunteered. ''I know the way, and won't anybody much bother about me doin' it.''

''Thanks, Dewey,'' Ellen said, scowling at Willie.

''Best I come along,'' Willie grumbled. ''Anyway, they'll need my horse to get along home.''

''Glad of the company,'' Dewey said, managing a smile.

''Sure,'' Willie muttered. ''Joe, you watch out for them.''

''Trust me to know what to do,'' the Cheyenne answered.

Willie and Dewey then solemnly loaded the bodies into the wagon. Ellen climbed atop Joe's pinto, for he had already mounted the gray, fearing it too much for her. Willie could have told Joe Ellen could ride anything with four feet. Billy and Cobb rode Dewey's paint, while Anne sat on

Joe's lap. Ellis climbed up on the pinto and clung to his mother's back.

"I'll have some dinner waiting," Ellen promised, as Joe led the way to the crossing. "Don't be long."

"Not a job to make a man tary," Willie answered. "We'll hurry it along."

CHAPTER 10

Willie and Dewey wasted little time transporting their grim cargo into Esperanza. Almost the moment they rolled down Front Street, a cry went up. Mills's hands collected outside the jail where Willie stopped the wagon.

"Look there," a cowboy named Clancy Long cried. "It's ole Fisher he's got there. Best trail cook I ever knew."

"Blake Lindsay's there, too," another cowboy noted.

"Lord, they were both at the river," Long said, shuddering. "And young Blake, why, he never so much as fired off a shot."

"This Rucker fellow's the very devil," Thurman Livingston declared, as he ordered the bodies unloaded. "How'd he know where to find 'em? I sent this batch to the line camp myself."

"And how'd he know who was there in the first place?" Mills asked, as he joined the group.

"I got some worse news, too," Livingston added. "Sheriff over in Albany wired this morning that Abel Meeks got himself stabbed last night."

Livingston and Mills exchanged anxious glances, then hurried the men back to their assigned tasks.

"Got a lot of men in town, it'd seem," Willie observed, as he prepared to turn the wagon back toward Salt Fork Crossing.

"Sent for help after that business at the school," Mills explained. "So I don't suppose I needed you after all, Fletcher. Truth is, I've a mind to send some men out looking for Rucker and his boys tomorrow. We're certain to pick up their trail and bring them to bay."

"And that'll be when you best start to worry," Willie told the rancher. "I wouldn't guess there's too many fellows left who rode to the river with you. How many? Two? Three?"

"One less," Long announced, stepping nervously over to Mills. "Boss, I got a bad feelin' comin' over me."

"Scared?" Livingston asked.

"Plenty," Long confessed. "I had a hand in what happened. Why, that fool Meeks told half of Esperanza was me dropped those boys. They'll be after me, sure."

"Rest easy," Mills said, taking the cowboy aside. "You're safe enough at the bunkhouse."

"I ain't safe anywhere in Texas," Long complained. "I heard o' that Rucker. He spent a month chasin' down a man who stole one o' his horses. Cut him to pieces down in Tuscan. I got a sister in Louisiana. I aim to get there quick as I can."

"Well, do as you think best," Mills grumbled. "Here's five dollars to hurry you along."

"Thank you, Mr. Mills, but could you make it ten?" Long asked. "I lost heavy Saturday night at the poker table."

"Here," Mills said, passing along another five. "Now, Thurm, what would you say to organizing a posse or two? Deputize men, and get them out early tomorrow morning."

"We could use that Indian tracker Fletcher's got workin' for him," Livingston said, nodding.

"Joe's got his own business to attend," Willie replied.

"And I got mine. Time we were heading on, Dewey. Climb on."

Dewey had been off gabbing with his uncle. Now the boy trotted back to the wagon and climbed onto the seat beside Willie.

"Posse's a fair notion," Dewey said, as the wagon rumbled along. "You aim to join up, Wil?"

Willie didn't answer. In fact he didn't reply to any of the three dozen questions Dewey asked on the long ride back to Salt Fork Crossing.

"But don't you figure we got an obligation of sorts?" Dewey exclaimed, as the wagon finally approached the river.

"Only obligation I know's to look after my own business," Willie muttered.

"You can't be forgettin' those Mills boys, Wil. After all, we both stuck our necks out mighty far at the school."

"That was for Ellie and the little ones," Willie argued.

"Are they safe now? The town's in danger. Esperanza. My town. Yours."

"Not mine, Dewey."

"I don't see how you can just ignore that Rucker fellow."

"I'm not," Willie answered. "Truth is, I'll keep my eyes open, but I don't altogether fault Riley for what he's done. You weren't at the river that day when Joe and I buried his nephew. Polk wasn't much older'n you, Dewey, and nigh as tall. I expect I'd call somebody to account if that happened to Billy or Cobb."

"Or me?"

"Sure. If they shot you full of holes, I'd be properly peeved."

"Wouldn't like it much myself, you know."

"Anyway, as I see it, Riley's after a sort of justice in his way. I don't have to agree with it to stand clear. But to take Mills' side, well, that'd be going along with what happened to Polk. I can't do that."

"And you'll just forget about this mornin'?"

"Riley let Ellie and the kids go, didn't he? Shoot, he didn't do more'n tear Jake's shirt a bit."

"He didn't stop with that," Dewey said, glancing back at the bloodstained wagon bed.

"No, and that won't be the end, either. Still, my hope's that Mills and the Ruckers'll square off and have at each other."

"Be a world of killin' come of it."

"Hope not," Willie said, as he halted the wagon outside the house. "But the trouble with a war's the bad habit it has of spreading. Like a plague sometimes."

Over a dinner of ham slices and biscuits, Willie listened to Ellen's views of the trouble.

"Won't this country ever know some peace?" she asked. "Last autumn it seemed we were making real progress. We had a church, a school, a real town. Now the preacher's left and the school's closed."

"Nobody much is left, anyway," Willie noted. "Most of the people took off for California."

"It's a sad day," Ellen said, sighing.

"We've known sadder," Willie observed. "Anyway, this trouble is certain to pass. Won't be any need to go back into Esperanza for a while, so it's best you just stick close to here. Might even consider visiting Trav down on the Clear Fork for a time."

"And what will you do?" she asked.

"I've got horses penned up and ready to work, remember? Soon as I chomp this last bite of biscuit, I aim to get after those ponies."

"Maybe you should stay with us," Billy said, looking warily into Willie's eyes. "Those men could come here."

"They weren't after you, son," Willie argued. "But if it'd comfort you, I could have Joe stay."

"You couldn't keep him away from those mustangs with leg irons," Ellen declared. "Right, Joe?"

The Cheyenne laughed his agreement, and Ellen began clearing away the plates.

"We won't be far," Willie assured her and the little ones. "An hour's hard ride. And we'll be by now and then."

"I'm not exactly helpless," Ellen countered. "Not with my boys around."

"And a shotgun handy," Billy added, grinning.

"Of course, you might consider staying on permanent, Willie," Ellen told him.

"We've spoken on this," he answered. "Not time yet."

"Will it ever be?" she complained. "Well, if you're determined to leave, get along with you, and leave me to my chores."

"Sure," Willie said, giving each of the little ones a comforting pat on the back before leaving. As he headed for the gray, Billy and Cobb raced out to block the path.

"We've done some growing lately," Billy said. "Maybe you could use some extra hands."

"I could, only who'd see your mama through the last of winter?" Willie asked. "And you've got chores here, don't you? Lessons?"

"They could wait a week," Billy grumbled.

"Hogs need feeding every day," Willie argued. "The time'll come when I take you two along soon enough. You grow fast enough without hurrying yourselves any."

"Told you he wouldn't take us," Cobb said, frowning.

"Never hurts to ask," Billy explained. "Might've taken us if it wasn't for those men at the school. He worries after Mama, you know."

Willie found himself smiling. Joe and Dewey walked past on their way to the horses, and Willie turned to join them. Moments later, the three of them were headed back toward the canyon.

The balance of the day Willie passed working the wildness out of a pair of mustangs. Joe worked another two, and

Dewey struggled with a fifth. It was slow going anytime, but on toward dusk the black stallion appeared, screaming defiantly and urging its harem to escape.

The solid rails of the fence thwarted any such attempt, but the mares pranced anxiously and whined their displeasure.

"By and by I want to build a corral down by the river," Willie told Joe, as they stoked the fire. "We can take ten of the likeliest ponies down there and work 'em."

"Closer to the crossin', you mean," Joe answered. "Sure, we can do it easy enough."

"And later on, I aim to have another try at that black demon," Willie added.

"Knew that," Joe said, grinning. "Just natural for two wild things to draw each other."

"Think I'm as wild as that horse, do you, Joe? Dewey?"

"Near as wild," Dewey said, grinning.

Willie clamped an arm over the youngster's head and wrestled him to the ground. Dewey squirmed a bit before wriggling free.

"Better hurry supper, Joe," Willie urged. "Poor Dewey here's down to bone with a little skin stretched over it."

"I keep eatin' Joe's cookin', I'll be even skinnier," Dewey complained. "Maybe we ought to ride down and beg Miz Trent out o' some biscuits."

"She's been troubled enough with us," Willie chided, and a hush fell over them that lasted halfway through dinner.

In truth it was near nightfall before things returned to normal. Joe was busy spreading his blankets beside the fire, while Willie collected twigs and brush for kindling.

"You always go to bed so early, Joe?" Dewey asked, as he sat beside the fire.

"Ain't been civilized enough to forget all my Cheyenne habits," Joe explained. "I go to sleep with the sun and get up with her."

"I used to do that when I was livin' with my Uncle Sime," Dewey said, sighing. "I miss those days."

"Aren't we treating you fair?" Willie asked. "Or did you have trouble with Rupe?"

"Neither," Dewey answered. "It's just that, well, I miss my cousins. I can't abide the quiet out here, or at Uncle Rupe's store. Back on the farm somebody was always stirrin'."

"Sure," Willie said, nodding. "That's how it is when we stay with the Trents. Half the time you wind up with a boy sleeping beside your bed, or else little Annie's waking you at first light to hear her prayers."

"It's just too blamed quiet!" Dewey growled.

"Not quiet at all," Willie argued. "Listen."

They sat silently for a few minutes. Gradually the sounds let themselves be heard. A chill wind whined across the forlorn landscape, while rabbits stirred near the fence. The horses stomped around, and bobwhites scurried about in a thicket.

"I hear," Dewey admitted.

"A man can find comfort in the stillness and solitude, but he still wants sounds now and again," Willie declared.

"They offer their own comforts, don't they?"

"Do indeed."

It was only with the spreading darkness that Willie noticed a pinprick of light a mile or so away on Blood Mesa. At first he wasn't sure it was real, for it came and went. In the end, though, he satisfied himself it was no haunt or spirit.

Riley's up there, Willie told himself.

Why not? Blood Mesa offered a perfect vantage point from which to view the nearby countryside. And the boulders and caves offered a hundred places to hide.

"That them?" Dewey whispered as he rolled out his blanket.

"Might be," Willie answered.

"You really think it likely we can dodge this trouble?"

"I hope so," Willie said, sighing as he spread his blankets opposite Dewey. "I've known my share of trouble."

"Me, too," Dewey whispered. "But that never kept more from comin' along."

CHAPTER 11

Willie enjoyed no peace that night. Again and again he saw Riley Rucker riding across the familiar hills along Salt Fork. And each time Riley's eyes held the same fiery anger as when he'd threatened young Jake Mills at the school.

"I'll be back!" Riley had warned then. Now those words seemed to stalk Willie like phantoms, plaguing him every moment.

Haven't you learned anything from the war? Willie silently asked his old comrade. Why are you rushing into battle all over again?

Willie's thoughts were flooded with ghastly scenes, and he shivered from a cold not brought on by any winter chill.

For a time he lay beside the embers of the fire, listening to Joe's snores and Dewey's labored breathing. That boy was troubled, too. Willie stared overhead as a full moon crept in and out of clouds. It was a fine night for hunting.

"That why you're here, Riley?" Willie whispered to the mesa. "Hunting Mills?"

Only the wind answered, and its ghostly wail provided little comfort.

Willie did manage a brief rest in the hours before **dawn**. Once the sun rose, though, he was awakened by the sounds of Joe preparing breakfast. First slabs of smoked bacon hit the hot bottom of a cast-iron skillet. Afterward, grease spattered here and there as Joe turned the sizzling strips.

"Griddle cakes again?" Dewey moaned, as he crawled out of his blankets and rubbed his eyes.

"You can always saddle your horse and ride back to the crossin' for some eggs," Joe replied. "Or try your own hand at the skillet."

"No thanks," Willie said, rubbing life into his numb legs. "I've tasted Dewey's efforts. Rather chew mesquite thorns."

"It wasn't *that* bad," Dewey objected.

"It's for sure nobody in your family's got fat from it," Joe observed. "Now hush up and get them blankets up and out o' the way. Man'd think you two were plannin' on sleepin' through the mornin'."

"No, just through the rest of the night," Dewey muttered.

"No use arguing," Willie said, as he rolled his blankets. "Man's hardheaded to a fault."

"Don't see why you keep him around," Dewey said loudly. The boy grinned as he turned away from Joe's harsh stare.

"He does cook good bacon," Willie confessed, "even if he is hard to get along with."

"Snores, too," Dewey added.

"I got a sharp knife for the next one with somethin' to say," Joe announced, pointing to his boot. "Well?"

"Not me, Joe," Dewey said, shaking his head as he stowed his bedding.

"Major?"

"Now what would I have to say?" Willie asked in turn.

"I think all white people must be crazed in the mornin'," Joe grumbled. "I'd be better off to head back to the plains."

"No buffalo left up there, Joe," Willie said sadly. "And

Custer's already been killed. Just gold miners and railway folks carving up the territories. And soldiers eager to murder Indians.''

By the time Willie put his blankets away, Joe had three plates stacked with griddle cakes and bacon. Coffee bubbled in a pot atop a bed of coals, and Willie began filling cups. Soon the mustangers were quietly eating their breakfast and watching a huge orange sun paint the eastern sky.

"Man above did a fine job o' things," Joe observed, as the morning daylight illuminated the rocky plain.

"If only man below could manage half as well," Willie added bitterly.

That was when he first noticed the riders on Blood Mesa. There were six or seven shadowy figures making their way down the slope a mile or so away. It was too far to make out faces, and not light enough, either. They were headed east, though, toward the river.

"Mills ain't livin' out that way," Joe noted, sitting beside Willie and staring at the riders with concern.

"Esperanza's the other way, too," Dewey declared. "I can't say I recall anything but cattle range north of the Salt Fork and east. Short of Young County, anyway."

"The crossing's out there," Willie observed. "Mills gets his supplies over that road."

"Not the middle of March yet," Dewey explained. "He gets what he needs from Uncle Rupe this time of the month."

"Then what's he after?" Willie asked, growing fearful over Ellen and the children.

"Eastbound stage leaves Esperanza this mornin'," Dewey said, trembling as he spooned the last of his breakfast into his mouth.

"Mills'd be scared some today," Joe suggested. "Might try to send some gold east to safety. Send for help, too."

"Could be passengers on that coach, as well," Dewey added. "If it was me, I'd get my womenfolk clear o' this business."

"Either way, the best spot to stop the coach is when it makes its crossing of the river," Willie pointed out. "That'd put Ellie smack in the middle of things."

"I'll saddle my horse," Dewey announced, setting his plate beside the fire and hurrying off.

"You douse the fire, Joe," Willie said, doing likewise. "I'll have your pinto waiting."

In a matter of minutes the three of them were riding east, threading their way across the rough country in an effort to cut off Rucker's men. All along the way Willie did his best to dissuade Dewey from coming along, but the sixteen-year-old insisted.

"I may not be all haired over like you, Wil, but I been walkin' my own path a while now. Joe there's got no whiskers, and you don't treat him like a boy! I proved I could fight, remember?"

"I remember more'n I want," Willie growled. "I'd spare you that, but like you say. It's your trail to ride."

"I've taken meals aplenty at Miz Trent's, and I got cousins I don't know as well as Billy. I helped put that house up, too."

"Guess you got a right to make it your fight, then," Willie agreed.

But when they finally crested the low hill leading to the crossing, they saw no stage. Joe had a look at the road and found no trace of wagon wheels.

"Backtrack," Willie announced, and they turned west.

As it happened, Riley Rucker had halted the stage a full mile short of the river. A pair of pistol shots warned Willie of what had happened, and he cautiously slowed the pace.

"It's good to be careful," Joe told an eager Dewey Hamer. "I had my fill o' ridin' into ambushes."

They caught sight of the coach moments later. Someone had unhitched the team and run the horses off. The stage stood at a bend of the road, its doors open and bundles of clothing scattered across the road. A money chest lay in the sand, its contents on their way elsewhere. The driver sat beside the front right wheel, cradling a busted arm. No one else was in sight.

"Wait here," Willie told his companions, as he pulled the gray to a stop and climbed down. Joe nodded, then drew his Winchester from its scabbard. Dewey fetched his rifle, too, but he wasn't about to stay behind. He followed a step behind Willie.

"Who's that?" the driver called in alarm, as Willie emerged from cover.

"Wil Fletcher," Willie answered. "You the only one aboard?"

"Got five passengers," the driver said, wincing as he moved his arm. "In the ravine yonder."

"Any of the ones that did it still around?" Willie asked.

"No, they lit out once they had the money," the driver added. "Marshal, you suppose you could have a look at my arm?"

"I'm not a marshal anymore," Willie replied.

"And there's somebody needs help worse'n you, Hopper," a somber-faced man in his mid-twenties, dressed in a banker's suit with the pockets torn out, declared.

Willie found two women and a boy of nine or so cowering in the ravine. Nearby, a cowboy lay sprawled beside a boulder. A pair of bullets had pierced his belly, and he was bleeding out his life.

"It's Clancy Long," Dewey said, turning away from the wounded man.

"Was your old friend Rucker!" Long cried. "Curse his hide, and yours for knowin' him!"

"Why'd you take 'em on?" Willie asked. "He was after the money. To hurt Mills."

"Maybe he wanted the money. Maybe not," Long said, coughing blood. "But mostly he wanted me. I was at the river, you see."

"I heard," Willie said, sitting beside Long and having a

look at the wounds. They were deep and clearly fatal. The cowboy had just moments left.

"Guess most o' the town knew," Long muttered. "Well, I done things I ain't proud of, and shootin' them boys is one. Should've been hung years ago. But I never earned bein' gut-shot and left to suffer. No, sir."

"He begged them to finish him," the banker explained. "But they just laughed. 'Maybe Mills'll do it,' the leader said."

"At least he spared us," one of the women said, clutching the boy to her side. "Was even kind to little Jeff here."

"Gave me stick candy," the boy said, showing it to Willie.

"Scared us to distraction, though," the second woman added. "And now we're stranded out here."

"Joe!" Willie shouted, and the Cheyenne appeared, rifle in hand.

"What next?" the first woman cried. "Indians!"

"I've seen this one around, Mrs. Kent," the banker said, walking over to her side. "He's tame."

"Not tame exactly," Willie argued. "But your scalp's safe."

Little Jeff seemed disappointed, but his mother was considerably relieved to discover Joe offered no harm.

"Best ride into Esperanza and fetch some help," Willie instructed. "Fresh horses for the stage, and a wagon to carry the driver and Long there back to town."

"Be faster to the Trent place," Joe pointed out.

"She's got no team for the stage. I expect we can take the passengers there, though, once—"

"Once I've died," Long said, trying to laugh. "Never expected to delay you folks on your journey. Hope you'll pardon me, as it's not exactly my doin'."

"Mr. Long, don't fret on it," Mrs. Kent said compassionately.

"Can you tell us how they did it?" Dewey asked, as he began splinting the driver's arm.

"All too easy," Hopper said, frowning. "Had two men out in the road when I slowed to take the turn. The rest come up on both flanks and from the rear. I hardly got the brake pulled when one threw a rope over my shoulders and drug me to the ground. That's when I busted my arm."

"They knew about the money," the banker, who introduced himself as Calvin Matthews, explained. "And where it was hidden below the seats. Mr. Mills had close to twenty thousand dollars in that box."

"Twenty thousand!" Dewey exclaimed.

"Most of his funds," Matthews continued. "All gone now. And no sooner did they take the money than they hauled that poor cowboy out behind the coach and shot him."

"Searched us, too," Mrs. Kent explained with a shudder. "I felt certain they planned to steal my locket, but they merely disarmed us. Flora had a pocket Colt, you see, and Mr. Matthews was carrying a side arm."

"Took two shotguns I had up top as well," Hopper said, grimacing as Dewey tightened the bindings on his arm. "If I'd gotten to them, it would've been a different story."

"Sure, Hopper," Matthews agreed. "You'd be dead."

"Mr. Matthews!" Mrs. Kent exclaimed.

"It's the truth," Matthews insisted. "As it is, they only took the money and shot poor Long there."

"That's not all they wanted, though," Long said, shivering as his eyes began to water. "Where've you got to, Fletcher? I can't see!"

"I'm close by," Willie said, reaching out and gripping the dying man's hand.

"They wanted to know about Mr. Mills and the sheriff," Long explained. "What their habits were."

"And you told 'em?" Willie asked.

"Now what would I know about the boss and that Livingston fellow?" Long asked, managing a chuckle. "I been a dust-eatin' drover all my days. Since I can remember, anyhow. I told 'em nothin'. Why would I? They left me gut-shot, didn't they?''

"There's something else, though," Willie said, reading the cowboy's eyes. "Tell me."

"Warn Hutchison," Long whispered. "They'll be after him next."

"Another of Mills' hands?" Willie asked.

"Wyatt Hutchison," Dewey said, growing pale. "Just a little older'n me. You'd remember his kin, Wil. The Dowes."

"Ought to," Willie said, scowling. "I buried some of them."

"Hutch wouldn't shoot anybody!" Dewey argued.

"Warn him," Long said, trying to sit up. He grew faint then and collapsed. His chest rose and fell, then was still.

"Pity I didn't know him any better," Matthews said, offering a blanket to cover the cowboy. "Seemed a good sort. I've seen men holler their heads off dying slow like that."

"Me, too," Willie admitted. "In the war."

"What now?" Dewey asked.

"I guess we could take the folks back to Ellie's," Willie said, standing. "Or wait for Joe."

"You said you sent to Esperanza for a wagon, didn't you?" Matthews asked. "Or was it for fresh horses?"

"I know Ellen Trent's place," Hopper announced. "It's miles away."

"We'll wait," Mrs. Kent said, frowning. "Flora's certainly not well enough for such a long walk."

"I could bring back horses," Dewey offered.

"I don't ride horses, young man," Mrs. Kent answered.

"I'm sure not waiting for any wagon back to Esperanza," Matthews declared. "Wasn't just Mills those riders wanted. They had a fair number of words for the town. No, I'm continuing eastward."

"I'll get you to Miz Trent's, if you don't mind ridin'

double," Dewey said. "You could wait there for the stage. Climb up, if you want."

"I'm grateful, son," Matthews said, following Dewey to where the paint stood grazing beside the road.

"Be back quick as I can," Dewey promised, as he mounted his pony. Matthews climbed atop, too, and the two of them headed east to Salt Fork Crossing.

When Dewey returned, he had company. Willie was more than a little surprised to see Abner Mills and his boy Albert there. Sheriff Livingston and a small band of men followed.

"I suppose Dewey's told you," Willie said, glancing down at the blanket covering Long's corpse.

"Grave news," Mills said sourly. "And they've taken my money as well!"

"There's another man in danger, too," Willie noted. "Wyatt Hutchison."

"We went fishing some," Albert said, trembling.

"Just a boy," Livingston added. "Well, Hutch's past carin' now. We come across him hangin' from a willow limb up by Tonkawa Creek."

"Just two left then," Willie observed, staring at Mills and Livingston.

"Two?" Mills asked. "No, I figure ten. Or were there more of them, ladies?"

"Ten's about right," Jeff answered. "You goin' after 'em, Sheriff?"

"We'll bring 'em to justice quick enough," Livingston boasted. "Right, Mr. Mills?"

"Right as rain," the rancher agreed.

Livingston then spurred his horse into a gallop, and the others followed in a swirl of dust. Willie turned away from them and rubbed the grit from his eyes. The ladies shook their fists in anger and coughed themselves half to death.

A half hour later Joe returned with a relief driver, a wagon, and the extra horses requested. Mrs. Kent drove the wagon back to Esperanza. Her boy Jeff was sandwiched between his mother and the pale Flora.

"We're heading along to Albany, ma'am," the new driver, Pete Perkins, had explained.

"I've had quite enough travel for one day, thank you," Mrs. Kent had answered.

And so Hopper had climbed into the back alongside Clancy Long's corpse, and the wagon began bouncing its way into Esperanza.

Willie helped Perkins get the horses hitched to the coach. As the stage set off eastward, Dewey led his horse over. A fretful look filled the sixteen-year-old's face.

"Dewey?" Willie called.

"Was talkin' to that banker Matthews," Dewey explained. "He says the Ruckers talked about burnin' Esperanza to the ground. The whole town. Uncle Rupe's there, Wil!"

"Best we have a look into things," Willie said, frowning. "I won't tell you to stay, Dewey, 'cause you wouldn't. But this time you stay back and leave me to call the play, understand? I want no new grief."

"Glad to let you lead, Major," Dewey responded.

"Joe, you hang back, too."

"I ain't got an eager bone to my body," the Cheyenne replied. "If you ask me, there's more'n one town ought to be burned down."

"My uncle's there!" Dewey cried.

"Didn't mean he should go with it," Joe said, dropping his gaze. "And we ain't gettin' there jawin' away like this."

"Then I guess we'd better do some riding," Willie said, slapping the gray into a gallop. The others followed, and soon they were hurrying toward Esperanza.

CHAPTER 12

Willie rode swiftly down the dusty road toward Esperanza. Behind him Joe Eagle and Dewey Hamer struggled to keep pace. The horses were all wearing down. Even the big gray was showing the strain of so much urgent riding.

Willie noted the horse's labored breathing and eased the pace. Shortly the faint outline of Esperanza appeared, and the riders slowed so as to make a cautious approach.

"I smell smoke!" Dewey shouted. "Look!"

Willie, too, sniffed an odor of burning planks on the wind, and he now spied a thick black plume rising from the far side of town.

"We'll leave the horses and go ahead on foot," Willie declared, swinging off the road and keeping the two-story Hamer mercantile between himself and Front Street.

"I mean to go ahead," Dewey announced, as he spurred his horse into a gallop. The youngster flew down the road, then jumped down and raced into his uncle's store.

Willie knew too well the cost of such foolhardy charges. He and Joe left their horses behind the Hamer corral and continued on foot. Willie had his pistol ready, and Joe carried his rifle. They crept along the side of the mercantile, then paused.

"I'll have a look," Willie explained, as he turned the corner and gazed through the open front door. The place was in total disarray, with goods scattered everywhere. Broken glass littered the floor. A bearded man in his mid-thirties stood beside the counter. On the floor beside him lay Dewey Hamer.

"I asked you your name, boy!" the man screamed, as he kicked Dewey's side.

"Hamer!" Dewey cried, hugging himself. "What've you done to Uncle Rupe?"

"The storekeeper," a second, younger man said as he emptied the Hamer cash box onto the counter. "He's not one of that rancher's brood. Too old, and far too thin. Those boys eat real fine, Lem. You kin of the storekeeper, eh? He got any other money? There's less'n thirty dollars here."

"Not much business this time of year," Dewey said, wincing as pain shot up his back. "You haven't hurt Uncle Rupe?"

"His good fortune to be elsewhere," Lem explained. "We got a powerful dislike for this town, what with people here murderin' my brother. I might just've shot him."

"Got good reason," the younger man added. "I'm Judson Driscoll. My baby brother's buried down on the river, shot as a rustler when he was bound for a cattle camp down south. You got brothers?"

"Cousins," Dewey said, backing away from Driscoll's angry eyes.

"Davey once rode thirty miles in a hailstorm to return a borrowed horse. He was ten years old at the time. Sound like a cow thief to you?"

"No, sir," Dewey answered. "Mister, I never shot 'em, and I got no use for Mills or his paid-for sheriff, either one. My uncle never brought you grief, either. It's for him I came, and that's my only worry."

"I'm your only worry," Lem argued, drawing a knife from his boot. "Where's Mills got to?"

"He came along after you robbed the stage," Dewey told them. "Headed to his ranch, I guess. Not to town."

"Tell Rucker," Lem growled. "I'll tend to this one personal."

Driscoll started for the door, and Willie stepped aside. When Driscoll passed through the door, Willie slammed his pistol barrel across the back of the young man's head and dropped him like a rock.

"Jud?" Lem called, when he heard Driscoll hit the ground.

"Drop the knife," Willie ordered, as he darted inside. The big man started toward Dewey instead, and Willie fired his revolver twice. Lem gazed in surprise as the second shot tore a hole in his chest. Blood spread in a bright scarlet circle until it stained the bearded man's whole shirt. Even so, Lem managed to lunge in Dewey's direction. A third shot snapped Lem's head back and knocked him to the floor.

"Lord, Wil, Uncle Rupe's gone," Dewey mumbled, as he slowly pulled himself to his feet. "I ran right into the middle of 'em. One got away."

"No he didn't," Willie said, nodding toward the door. "Now, you plan to listen to what I say from now on?"

"It's apt to prove safer," Joe added, joining them inside the store.

"And if I don't?" Dewey asked.

"I'll hog-tie you, throw you on my horse, and send it back to the river," Willie said, staring hard at the youngster. Willie's gaze softened when Dewey opened his shirt and showed a patch of purple where Lem's toe had struck.

"Got a rib cracked there," Joe said, stepping closer. "Sit down and let me have a good look."

"You a medicine man?" Dewey asked, nervously peering out the side window.

"Closest thing to one you got around here," Joe replied. "Major, might be you should have a look outside. Them shots have a bad habit of drawing crowds."

"I'll be over at the school," Willie said, stepping back to the door. Front Street remained deserted, so Willie ran across to the school. A pair of desks were shoved back from one window. Otherwise it was as Ellen had left it.

Willie waved to Joe, then continued across to the abandoned church. It, too, was empty. Up the street, though, there was plenty of life. Warren Rucker and a younger boy were carrying flour sacks out of the hotel. Across the way smoke poured from the bank. A pair of cowboys were pouring coal oil onto the steps of the town hall, and a third man applied a torch when they'd finished.

"So much for Granny Gunnerson's dream," Willie muttered, as flames licked at the building. Soon the whole town was certain to go the same way. Warren seemed mainly interested in the hotel, but others looted the shops of whatever struck their fancy. One man led several horses out of the livery stable. Another threw a chair through the window of the barbershop. A small boy raced out the door, but was cut off by Riley Rucker himself just outside the hotel.

"Pa!" the boy screamed. "Help me!"

"What's your name, boy?" Riley said, grabbing the boy by his shoulders and shaking him violently.

"Rodney," the youngster answered. "Rodney Hays."

"Hays, huh? And who'd your daddy be?"

"Jim Hays," Rodney explained. "Runs the stable."

"Don't run it anymore," Warren said coldly. "He was in the hotel."

"He's dead," Riley said, and Rodney crumpled like a rag doll. "Now, what do you know about Mills and the sheriff?"

"Leave him be!" Agnes Keller exclaimed, running over from the telegraph office. "He's just a child. The town bootblack. He doesn't know anything!"

"And what do you know, lady?" Riley said, turning to confront the woman.

"I cook at the hotel," she answered. "I was told not to prepare a midday meal. Mr. Mills planned to eat at his

104

ranch, I believe, and the sheriff was off with his posse."

"That sheriff couldn't find water on a rainy day," Riley complained. "If he was up to his job, he'd never've shot my nephew."

"If your nephew was anything like you, sir, the sheriff did his duty!" Agnes retorted, as she helped little Rod Hays up from the ground. "Even divine mercy won't spare you eternal damnation for what's gone on today."

"And what'll spare you, lady?" Riley asked, waving a pistol in the air. "I take it in my head to shoot you, will some angel happen along to save you? Won't happen, will it, boy?"

"Angels been busy hereabouts lately," Rodney muttered. "Took my ma just after Christmas and my little sister last month. Now my pa. You go ahead and shoot me if you like, but leave her be. She done you no harm."

"Brave little cuss," Warren observed.

"I'm sorry about your pa," Riley said, changing his tone. "We went into the hotel quick, and there was some shootin'. Three men got kilt there, and your pa had the bad luck to be one. You got kin?"

"Aunt in Austin," Rodney explained.

"Warren, give the cook some money so she can see he gets there safe," Riley ordered. "Then put 'em in a wagon and get 'em clear o' this place."

"What about the others?" Warren asked. "We got 'em collected back of the jail."

"Send 'em on their way," Riley answered. "We missed Mills again. That's clear enough."

Warren handed Agnes Keller a stack of greenbacks and led her and Rodney along toward the jail. She went rather freely. Rodney paused a moment, insisting he wanted to see his father.

"No you don't," Warren argued. "Trust me to know, boy. I seen my brother in my dreams, shot to pieces down at the river. I don't sleep without him visitin' my nightmares."

"What about the rest of the town, Mr. Rucker?" the cowboy with the coal oil called.

"Burn it," Riley commanded.

"It's not the town's fault!" Willie yelled from the cover of the church.

"Well, Major," Riley answered, stepping out into the open while the others scurried for shelter. "Figured you'd happen along sooner or later."

"People get their living here," Willie declared.

"I hear this is Mills' town. I owe him a roastin' in hell for what he's done. Just figure this is sort of a start."

"Where's Uncle Rupe?" Dewey shouted from the store.

"The people are down by the jail," Willie answered. "Boy's uncle owns the store there, Riley. He's a friend, and he's got no love of Abner Mills."

"Boy puts me in mind o' myself when I joined you and Ray up in Virginia," Riley said, frowning. "You ain't lost your knack for takin' in strays, eh?"

"Guess not," Willie answered. "Give Dewey leave to fetch his uncle home, and I'll stay on my side of the street here."

"No, Riley!" Judson Driscoll cried, struggling to step out from behind the mercantile. "He went and shot poor Lem Cranmers."

"You do that?" Riley asked.

"I shot somebody," Willie admitted. "Was ready to take a knife to Dewey there."

"Cracked me across the head, too," Driscoll added.

"Then you're lucky you ain't dead, Jud. This-here's the poor old soldier friend who kept your brother from the buzzards. Guess that tempers your complaint some."

"Then why's he takin' Mills' side?" Driscoll demanded.

"Didn't know I was," Willie responded. "Let Dewey fetch his uncle, will you?"

"He's in the hotel," Warren said sourly. "Not with the others."

Dewey broke into a run, and Willie watched anxiously as

106

the sixteen-year-old raced up Front Street and dashed inside the hotel. Dewey stayed but a moment. Then he stumbled out, his face pale as cotton.

"He was unlucky," Warren explained. "Standin' right next to the front desk. Fool clerk pulled a gun. Shotgun blast hit 'em both."

"He's dead," Dewey said, dropping to his knees. "Uncle Rupe's dead. Poor man never had a cross word for anybody, and he's lyin' in there murdered."

"Dewey, come on over here," Willie pleaded.

"Ain't leavin' Uncle Rupe," the boy vowed.

"Then you're apt to burn with him," Warren explained, prying Dewey from the door. The two teens stared at each other a moment. Then Dewey freed himself and stepped back inside.

"Help him pull the bodies out," Riley suggested, and a pair of men followed Warren into the hotel. They hauled out Rupert Hamer, Jim Hays, and the faceless desk clerk. Dewey tried to carry his uncle across to the church, but his sore ribs prevented it. Willie warily walked out into the street and took the dead man's legs. Dewey lifted Rupe Hamer's shoulders, and together they managed to make it over to the churchyard.

"You lookin' for any other favors, Major?" Riley asked.

"Just to be left alone," Willie answered.

"Yeah, I asked that myself a time or two. Ain't happened yet," Riley said, shaking his head. "Pray we don't meet again, Willie. I'm growin' short o' hands. From here on out I'm apt to shoot anybody."

"No time for talking, huh?"

"Not nowadays. And not with a snake like Mills. Stay clear o' yon mountain, too."

"Got horses there to work," Willie explained.

"Sure," Riley grumbled. "We all got things to do, don't we? Well, till better days, adios."

"Till better days," Willie echoed.

Twenty people stumbled out from behind the jail then,

led by Agnes and little Rodney. No sooner had they left than Rucker's men set the place afire. Likewise they made their way from building to building, burning each in its turn.

"Not the church!" Agnes pleaded, but it, too, was torched. Then the school went. Finally the men with torches turned to Hamer's store.

"That place never belonged to Mills!" Willie shouted.

"I mean to burn the whole town," Riley insisted. "Leave a black scar to mark its passin'."

"It's all the boy's got," Willie said, gazing into Dewey's distraught eyes. "And it was here before the town was."

"It goes," Riley barked. "As to the boy, he's got his life. That's more'n some have. You see Mills, tell him I'm not finished."

"Tell him yourself," Willie growled.

The store erupted in flames then, and the Ruckers rode away. Willie remained, sadly watching the town named for hope melt into memory.

"Uncle Rupe was your friend, Wil," Dewey managed to say before emotion overpowered him. "And you stood by while those murderers did this to him. And burned his store. It meant everything to him."

"No, it was just planks and nails and dry goods," Willie argued. "We talked about that when we rebuilt El-lie's place. Only things that really mattered were you and your cousins. He'd find solace knowing you were all right."

"Is that what I am?" Dewey said, as tears poured down his cheeks. "I feel half-dead."

"Least you're not all the way dead," Joe Eagle said, resting a leathery brown hand on the boy's shoulder. "I lost everybody in my family."

"Does it hurt less to lose *one*?" Dewey asked, dropping his face into his hands.

"No, a loss's a loss," Willie said, stepping over to a tool shed and grabbing a spade. "Young or old, kin or friend, the pain's always there. Lord, I've buried too many people in my lifetime! When's it going to stop?"

"Life's pain," Agnes said, leading little Rodney along to where his father rested, covered by a blanket.

"She's right," Willie agreed. "And for what it's worth, Rupe's free of that pain now. And the torments that life brings a man."

"It's little comfort," Dewey cried, lightly touching Rodney's shoulder. "To him, or to me. Tell me, Wil, what'll you do now? Is it still none of your business?"

"I'm going to bury a friend," Willie explained, as he plunged the spade into the rocky soil. "And help you if I can."

"Help me find justice for Uncle Rupe?" Dewey asked.

"Any way I can," Willie said solemnly.

CHAPTER 13

Esperanza blazed red and awful. Clouds of smoke and ash swallowed the sun, leaving the land cold and gray and heartless.

"It's fittin'," Dewey Hamer remarked as Willie sat beside the finished grave, fighting to catch his breath. Behind him the timbers of the church crashed to the ground, but that wasn't what etched the lines in his forehead. No, that was the killing. The toil and the hard riding had taken a toll, too. He was exhausted, and the very air now threatened to choke him.

"Sure," Willie said, frowning his agreement. "Funerals ought to be held on days this dark and cold."

"Can't be a funeral," Rodney Hays objected, as he stared at the holes made ready for his father and the desk clerk a few feet away. "We got no preacher."

"What good would he be?" Dewey complained bitterly. "Everybody here knew Uncle Rupe. Ain't a thing a preacher could say we don't know."

"Could offer words of comfort," Agnes Keller suggested, as Rodney clung to her side.

"What comfort's to be found in this godforsaken town?" Dewey cried. "Only death's come here lately."

"We need a preacher," Rodney repeated.

"We've got a Bible," Agnes assured the boy. "That'll do."

"Will have to," Willie agreed, as he tried to calm Dewey.

Agnes opened up her Bible and read from Revelations. She spoke of God, the beginning, and the end. She painted a picture of a world of eternal peace and beauty. It was her final remarks that struck Willie, though.

"But as for the cowardly, the faithless, the polluted, as for murderers, fornicators, sorcerers, idolaters, and all liars, their lot shall be in the lake that burns with fire and brimstone, which is the second death."

Gazing at the smoldering ruin that had been Esperanza, those words acquired fresh meaning. Indeed, it seemed Hell had arrived on earth.

"Or we've fallen into the pit itself," Dewey said afterward, as he shoveled dirt over his uncle.

"Does seem so," Willie agreed, as he brushed ashes from his coat. "Yup," he added, sniffing the air. "Sure enough smells of fire and brimstone."

It was a bit later, after the two of them had carved Rupert Hamer's name on the crude cross that marked the grave, that Willie led Dewey past the ashes of the store to where their horses restlessly waited.

"What now?" Dewey asked, as they walked.

"Don't know," Willie muttered, as he sat on a boulder. Taking a deep breath, he pulled his Colt revolver from its holster and emptied the chambers of its cylinder. He sighed, then rose and walked to the gray's side.

"Major?" Dewey asked.

"Got to see to your tools," Willie explained, as he withdrew a small leather case from his saddlebags. He returned to the boulder and began cleaning the pistol. He gritted his teeth and brushed powder grains and dust from each cylinder. He checked the firing pin and started on the barrel. Again and again he cleaned the gun.

"Wil?" Dewey said, resting a tired hand on his friend's back. "Don't you figure it's clean now?"

"Clean?" Willie cried. "No, you can't ever really get 'em clean, not once they been used."

"Oh?"

"Just like you can't get the powder smoke out of your nose, off your clothes, out of your eyes."

"I don't understand," Dewey said, sighing. "What's wrong?"

"I killed a man," Willie explained. "At your uncle's store."

"He was ready to kill me!" Dewey exclaimed. "You saved my life."

"Maybe," Willie mumbled. "But I was sure quick to do it, wasn't I? Could be that poor fellow had cause to be angry. I might've sneaked around him, given him a whack on the head like that other one."

"You'd've needed longer arms," Dewey declared. "He was pretty far away, and he'd have kilt me certain."

"Likely you're right," Willie admitted. "But it doesn't make it a particle easier to live with."

"I remember how it was when those Scarlet fellows attacked the crossin'. Your eyes got all dark, and you'd hardly talk to anyone. You said the madness had come back."

"Has again."

"I didn't understand then."

"And now?"

"I guess maybe I do," Dewey said, dropping his gaze. "Only last time it was simple. Those fellows were out to kill us, and we were fightin' back. Now . . ."

"It's all jumbled," Willie said with a frown. "Confused. Man I used to know like a brother came to town and did this," Willie added, waving toward the scarred landscape. "Killed a friend of mine. Likely you'll ask me to ride after him now, maybe shoot bullets into him."

"He killed Uncle Rupe."

"Or his men did. And why'd he do it, Dewey? Was on

account of his nephew being shot to pieces by that idiot Mills!"

Willie shivered, and Dewey fetched a blanket from his horse. Willie shook it away, though.

"Isn't the wind's chilled me to the bone," Willie explained. "It's the remembering. And knowing what's sure to follow."

Willie finished with the cleaning tools and returned them to their case. Then he holstered the Colt and stared northward toward the distant outline of Blood Mesa.

"This is how it was in the war, Dewey," Willie said with a sigh. "Day before battle. You'd make your tools ready, then try to muster enough stomach to do what you had to. Some couldn't do it. You'd see it on both sides, boys who'd join the charge with unloaded weapons. One had me in his sights once, only instead of shooting he only nodded and waited for me to drop him instead. Thing is, the killing eats a man's soul, and he gets so he doesn't care anymore."

"Not you!"

"Me? Plenty of times. But I was a major by then, and I owed my men. Had to lead the way."

"And after the war?"

"I found myself a mountaintop and tried to forget."

"Or a valley maybe, where you could work horses."

"Sure, and it close to worked this time," Willie said, coughing and fighting to shake off an aura of death.

"You know I aim to go after them," Dewey said, circling so as to face Willie. "If I asked you to come along, would you?"

"To bring your uncle's killers to justice? Or to kill Riley Rucker?"

"The two are the same, don't you think?"

"Likely are. Dewey, you'd be better served to forget your pain. It'll be easier to swallow than the fight you'll find. The death you'll see."

"I've seen plenty already."

"But you're determined to see more?"

Dewey nodded, and Willie shivered. Again Dewey offered the blanket, but Willie turned away. The rumble of approaching horsemen and a rolling wall of dust swept their attention toward the road.

"They've come back!" someone shouted from across the street, and the crowd at the churchyard sought what scant cover remained. Willie swallowed hard and turned to face the new trouble. He relaxed some as his ears picked up the notes of a mouth organ. Soon the dust cleared, and Abner Mills called a drunken greeting.

"What's happened to the town, Thurm?" Mills demanded. "The store was right here, wasn't it? I can't have drunk that much!"

"Somebody went and burned it all down," Sheriff Livingston observed, as he dismounted and kicked a blackened board that had once been part of the school. "Lord, they've burned the whole town!"

Others among the horsemen howled and hooted.

"Must've been a fine bonfire, that!" one of them shouted.

"This was all your doin'!" Dewey then hollered from across Front Street. "You killed that Rucker boy, and his uncle's kilt mine."

"Rupe's dead?" Livingston asked, sobering somewhat.

"And others," Willie added. "Desk clerk. Jim Hays."

"Got the hotel safe then," Mills muttered.

"I can see why he'd do that," Livingston added. "But why gun a stableman and a shopkeeper?"

"They were in the hotel," Agnes Keller said, fighting to hold back young Rodney. "Please, Rod, no."

But the boy broke loose and rushed to the rancher's side. Even as Mills was climbing down, Rodney drove a fist into the man's leg.

"You got my pa kilt!" the boy screamed.

"Settle yourself down," Sheriff Livingston said, dragging Rodney from Mills's side. "Now!"

"Let him loose," Agnes insisted, as she pried the lawman's hands from the youngster. "You know there's truth in what he says. I heard you talking about killing those boys at the river."

"Hold your tongue, Miss Keller, or you'll find yourself short of work," Mills replied.

"Why not?" Agnes barked. "I've lost everything I owned in the hotel. And what job would you have me do now?"

"I take care of my people," Mills argued, as he drew out his wallet. "First tell me what's happened here. Then we'll come to some sort of agreement. All of you!" Mills added, waving the cowering townsfolk nearer.

In short order Agnes narrated the tale. When she'd finished, Mills offered the men new jobs at the ranch and paid what he could toward replacing their lost belongings.

"I'm afraid there's little I can do for you, son," Mills told Dewey. "Your uncle didn't work for me."

"I don't want your money," Dewey growled.

"As for you, Rodney, I do feel—"

"I got some money," Rodney interrupted. "Them others give it to Agnes. And I'd rather take it from them, now I know about the river. Guess you'd shoot me, too, huh?"

"If you were rustling cows," Mills answered.

"This isn't about rustling," Willie said, staring at Mills with growing bitterness. "It's about murder. And coming to terms before this whole county's swimming in blood."

"Don't worry yourself over it, Fletcher," Livingston said, laughing. "We got plenty of men here eager to square accounts."

"And more at the ranch," Mills added. "At daybreak we'll pick up their trail and ride them into the dust."

"Why not now?" Dewey asked. "Trail's fresh."

"But we're not," Livingston said, pointing awkwardly to the dizzy assortment of hands sitting limply atop their horses. "Will be by first light."

"Thurm, send somebody to the ranch," Mills instructed. "Have wagons brought out for anyone who wants to go there. As for Miss Keller and anyone eager to go upon their way, the road awaits them.''

Mills then tottered toward a watering trough and managed to splash water onto his face. His skin had a greenish tint, and he soon retired behind what was left of the school and became sick.

"Where you goin'?" Dewey asked, as Willie turned toward his horse.

"Thought I'd borrow a horse off Rupe and get Agnes and the boy along to Salt Fork Crossing,'' Willie explained. "Might be the stage is still there. If not, well, there's another due before long.''

"You aren't going with Mills?" Dewey asked.

"With him?" Willie cried. "I look crazed in the head?"

"At least he plans to do somethin' about all this,'' Dewey said, kicking a charred barrel stave. "I guess I'll head out to his ranch.''

"Wish you wouldn't,'' Willie said, gazing intently into the sixteen-year-old's grief-stricken eyes. "It won't be what you expect, Dewey. Not with Mills. Could be he'll even get you killed.''

"I don't see how that'd be your worry.''

"Then you don't know me much,'' Willie answered angrily. "We shared camps, Dewey. Been mustanging.''

"And more,'' Dewey added. "Fought side by side. Now you're runnin' from my troubles, and I got to face 'em head on.''

"You've heard nothing I've said today.''

"Heard it all,'' Dewey argued. "But I suppose you'd say this is where I walk my own path.''

"Man comes to that point by and by,'' Willie admitted, offering his hand. "It'd be a comfort to know we parted friends, though.''

"A friend would ride along,'' Dewey muttered, as he turned and stomped away. Willie watched the boy take his horse and head for Mills. He stopped halfway and motioned toward the three horses milling around a small corral behind the ashes of the mercantile. "Miss Keller and Rod're welcome to the horses. I'll expect 'em to be at Miz Trent's."

"They'll be there," Willie promised. "As I will be, for a time. Should you come to have need of me."

"Got need now," Dewey said, pausing again. "Won't you—"

"I can't," Willie said, staring at his toes. The cold threatened to overwhelm him, and he staggered. Dewey nodded sadly, then continued onward. Willie meanwhile collected Agnes Keller and little Rod Hays. The Hamer horses lacked tack, but Rodney salvaged some from the gutted livery and saddled a gentle white mare for Agnes. He himself hopped atop a black gelding and rode the animal bareback.

"Lead the way, Marshal," Agnes suggested.

"I'm not a marshal nowadays," he replied.

"Better'n what's come after you," Rodney grumbled, and Willie tried to muster a smile for the boy. It wasn't possible, so instead Willie started up the road toward Salt Fork Crossing. He hoped the stage had delayed its crossing of the river. Best thing for Rodney Hays was to put some distance between himself and the nightmare world of Esperanza.

CHAPTER 14

The eastbound stage had been as eager to flee Esperanza as Willie, and by the time he and his two companions reached Salt Fork Crossing the coach was a long time gone. Nevertheless, Ellen offered what comforts she could to Agnes Keller—a hot bath and a change of clothes—while Billy and his brothers took charge of Rodney Hays. A bit later Joe Eagle, with Annie perched on his shoulders, located the boys and entertained them with Cheyenne games and stories.

"Watching them play, it's hard to imagine all that's happened," Ellen told Willie. "Esperanza gone! The whole town burned!"

"Yes, but it's just the beginning," Willie said, staring off toward Blood Mesa. "I've been considering things, and I think you should take Annie and the boys down to Clear Fork. Stay with Trav awhile."

"This is our home," Ellen objected.

"You can build a new house," Willie observed. "Hard to grow a new crop of kids."

"We've weathered worse."

"You didn't see Riley's eyes. As to Mills, well, he's not the most sensible man I ever knew when sober. Now he's taken to drink, who knows what'll come of things. A batch of liquored cowboys can do a lot of damage.''

"Don't you think I know all that?" Ellen asked. "We lived in Wichita during its heyday.''

"There was always law in Wichita, even in the worst times,'' Willie argued. "That Livingston may wear a badge, but he's as evenhanded as a copperhead. I wouldn't trust him to wipe my boots.''

"Neither side has cause to come here,'' Ellen pointed out.

"They might view it different.''

Ellen then led Willie down to the river. They strolled along the banks for close to an hour before she paused.

"You've said nothing about Dewey,'' she whispered. "I know the kinship you felt for that boy. He's come to no harm, I hope.''

"No holes in him, if that's what you mean,'' Willie replied. "Took Rupe's shooting hard, though. Joined up with Mills and his boys. Wouldn't even shake my hand.''

"That won't last,'' she assured him. "Pain passes, after all.''

"Or eats you up,'' Willie added. "Either way, you'll hold his horses here for him?''

"No trouble to that,'' she answered. "But then you'll be here to see after them.''

"Will I?'' he asked. "You know, Ellie, I can feel the winds of death on my back. I can smell it, the blood and the murder. It's close.''

"Maybe you could meet with Riley,'' she suggested. "Help him come to terms.''

"Not possible,'' he murmured. "I wouldn't be welcome among his company now, anyhow. I killed one of 'em in Hamer's store.''

"Agnes told me,'' Ellen said, wrapping an arm around his heavy shoulders.

"We should leave,'' he argued. "Take the little ones and run for our lives.''

"Haven't you learned anything these last fifteen years?" she cried. "You can't turn away from trouble and expect it to go away. It doesn't."

"No, it hangs around till it kills you!" he exclaimed. "You know, I'd almost welcome death. But I can't stand the thought of it finding you, or one of the little ones."

"Or Dewey?"

"Yeah, that eats at me some," Willie admitted. "Riley said I've got a bad habit of taking in strays. He's right about that. Can't help myself, though. I know what it's like to ride alone."

Willie was anything but alone that night, though. He, Joe, and little Rodney spread their blankets on the floor beside Billy, Cobb, and Ellis. The small room was filled with a mixture of Joe's snores, Rodney's thrashing, and the younger boys' less restless tossing. By midnight Billy had eased his way over so that his left arm rested against Willie's right leg, and by daybreak Cobb and Ellis were nigh as near. Rodney had nestled in beside Joe, who woke muttering about sneaky whites.

"He don't mean it," Rodney announced, leaning on Joe's sturdy frame. "Indians never say what's in their hearts. Pa taught me that."

"Your pa knew lots o' Cheyennes, did he?" Billy asked.

"Some," Rodney answered, sighing. "Wish he'd taught me more. But then he never had the time."

Willie nodded sadly and hurried to get dressed. Joe gave Rodney a tap on the back and followed suit. The boys did likewise and had their mother drop-jawed surprised to find blankets rolled against the wall and chores started when she called everyone to breakfast.

Halfway through ham and eggs Dewey Hamer arrived. Behind him Abner Mills and Thurman Livingston led a dozen armed cowboys. The rowdies shouted and fired off pistols until Willie stepped outside to greet them.

"We're headin' for Blood Mesa!" Livingston shouted. "You comin', Fletcher?"

"I'm having my breakfast," Willie replied.

"I told 'em where the Ruckers are," Dewey explained, turning to Willie with pleading eyes. "But they're in no fit condition to catch anybody nappin'."

Willie sniffed the air and nodded. Mills and his cohorts had already fortified themselves with whiskey.

"You don't know that mountain," Joe Eagle declared, as he stepped out beside Willie. Rodney Hays was at the Indian's side, and Joe gazed solemnly at the boy.

"It's a bushwhacker's paradise up there," Willie agreed. "Best you slow down, take it easy. And it's sure no place to take a boy."

That last comment was aimed at Abner Mills, whose boy Albert rode beside him. Albert was just thirteen, and on a good day he might have stretched five feet from toe to straw-colored hair.

"He'll be fine," Mills argued. "He's a Mills."

"Nearly paid the price for that at the school," Willie recounted. "You don't know what you're headed into with these fellows. Got 'em too fuzzy-headed to shoot straight, too."

"They'll sober up," Mills declared.

"Not if we're lucky," one of the cowboys remarked.

"You'll all of you be dead by nightfall," Willie said, frowning. "Dewey . . ."

"We do need a scout," Livingston said, nudging his horse over so as to stand between Mills and the house. "I know you've no heart for it, Fletcher, but your interests are at stake. They won't forget you kilt that fellow at the store. I know these people. They'll get their dander up, and if they finish us, be assured they'll not leave before payin' you a call."

Ellen and the children filled the door, and Willie eyed them soberly. There was truth in Livingston's words, and he wished they would head south. There was little hope of that.

"Best we go and finish this, Major," Joe suggested.

"Know where they are?" Willie asked.

"Got my notions," Joe confessed.

"It's agreed then," Livingston said, grinning. "I'll take Mr. Mills and his boys out to your horse camp at the base of the ridge. You and the Indian there scout the mountain. Take young Hamer with you. You can send him back once you spot the camp."

"Take Albert, too," Mills suggested. "Two riders are better than one."

"Dewey knows the way," Willie argued. "Besides, I'm no wet nurse."

"Please, Marshal," Albert whispered, riding out from the shadow of his father. "That Livingston makes me nervous."

"Why don't you head home?" Willie asked sourly.

"Can't do that," the boy answered. "I'm eldest, discounting Alice. It's a duty."

"Get yourself some growth," Willie advised.

"We all been that age, Major," Joe said, nodding toward Dewey. "Can't always be a left-behind."

"Lord, Joe, he's only a kid!"

"Bigger'n I was the first time I went on a war party," Joe said, laughing. "He'll be safe enough with us."

"You'll do just what I say?" Willie asked. Albert nodded, and Willie frowned. "Then come on," Willie added with a shrug. "Big mistake, Mills."

But Abner Mills wasn't paying heed. He'd already formed his men into a column. Now Livingston took the lead and galloped toward the box canyon.

"Some scouts," Willie muttered, as he stepped back inside the house, determined to finish his breakfast. "They'll have everyone on that mountain stirred up."

"Or put 'em at ease," Joe said, following Willie to the table. Ellen set places for Dewey and young Albert, and soon everyone was busy eating. Willie observed with some delight that Albert's manners soon yielded to appetite, and the thirteen-year-old dipped his biscuit in ham gravy like a natural-born Brazos boy.

"I'll pack up some food for you," Ellen announced when the last plate stood empty.

"I appreciate that," Willie answered. "We shouldn't be all that long."

"No, it doesn't take but a few minutes to kill," she said, swallowing bitter tears. "Strange that, considering dying's such a permanent thing."

Willie nodded, then clasped her hand as she walked to the stove.

"I'll be careful," he promised.

"No you won't," she told him. "I know you, Willie. You'll be in the thick of it. Well, you're you, and I wouldn't love you any other way, I suppose. Still, you're little use to me dead."

"Not much use to myself that way," he said, mustering a smile.

"Here," she said, handing him a flour sack full of dried beef, bread, and three tins of beans.

"I'll do my best to get back," Willie pledged. "Maybe then we can make some serious plans."

"I wish I could believe that," she said, rubbing her eyes. "But I've heard it before."

"Sure," Willie said, as he slung the bag over his shoulder. By the time he was outside, Joe had the big gray saddled and waiting. Dewey and Albert mounted their waiting animals, and Joe pulled himself atop his pinto.

"Just waitin' for you, Major," Joe announced.

Willie mounted and looked over his meager command. Yes, it was the war all over again. He was setting out with too few men, to do a job he didn't care for in the first place. With luck they could track the Ruckers unseen and get them surrounded. Even Riley could judge a hopeless position.

At first all went according to plan. Willie found the trail himself, and Joe traced it up the rocky slopes of Blood

Mesa. Later, dismounted, the four of them crept up the rugged mountain until they located a camp beside a bubbling spring on the mesa's western ridge.

"It's them," Dewey whispered, excitement creeping into his voice. Joe paled, and Willie frowned. Below them half a dozen men kept guard over four makeshift shelters. Inside, women scrubbed clothes and tended children. Riley Rucker and his men had brought along the whole community.

"Didn't trust leaving them behind," Willie noted. "We can't attack them here."

"Won't be a need," Dewey argued. "Once we have 'em surrounded, Rucker's sure to give up. He wouldn't risk all those children."

"Sure he won't," Albert agreed. There was something grim and unspoken in the boy's eyes, and Willie felt a chill creep through his insides.

"I'll fetch Mills," Dewey said, starting back toward the horses.

"Wait," Willie commanded. "Joe, maybe you'd best go along, make sure the others understand how it's to be done."

"Figure they'll listen to me?" Joe asked skeptically.

"There's a chance," Willie replied. "Anyway, they won't otherwise know where to ride."

"And once they get here?" Joe asked.

"We'll offer Rucker a chance to surrender," Dewey answered. "And if they won't, we'll shoot him down for the dog he is."

"Dewey?" Willie gasped, reading the fury in the young man's face.

"They kilt Uncle Rupe," Dewey pointed out. "Ain't any forgettin' that. Nor forgivin' it, either."

Joe and Dewey then turned toward the horses, and Willie made his way to a nest of boulders from which he could keep watch on the camp below. Albert settled in nearby, his nervous hands fumbling with a Remington revolver.

124

"I'd rather you put that pistol aside," Willie said, as he watched Riley embrace a tallish, dark-haired woman that could only be Rachel, his wife. Willie had visited them on his way back from Kansas in '78. There were five youngsters now, according to Warren. Willie recalled only the eldest, a sweet-faced girl named Leanna. She would be fourteen now. He spied her just past her mother, absorbed with tending a trio of boys no taller than Billy Trent.

Another time I'd be sitting down to supper with them, Willie thought. As things stood, he and Riley would soon face each other in bloody battle, with Rachel and the children right in the middle of it. Willie Delamer recalled such fights. He had little confidence in a peaceful resolution of affairs. Still, if he walked down there and spoke to Riley personally . . .

"Hold it, Mr. Fletcher," Albert warned, as Willie started to rise.

"Boy?" Willie asked, turning to find Albert poised with a cocked pistol.

"Pa said to watch you. You wouldn't want to give us away, would you?"

"Albert, I can draw and fire before you get off a second shot," Willie warned. "Maybe even a first."

"Maybe," Albert admitted. "Maybe not."

The boy's fingers trembled some, and so the aim was uncertain. Still, the range was so short that—

Horses reached the camp suddenly. There was no time for meeting with Riley Rucker or settling the feud peacefully. Mills and his boys hit the camp with wild abandon. Cowboys raced in, shooting anything that moved. Women screamed, and children fled for their very lives. Willie saw Rachel rush out to shield a small boy and fall to a pair of rifle shots. The boy at her side was cut down by Mills himself.

Nobody can be this insane! Willie screamed inside.

"Try to warn them now," Albert said, as he leaped down from the rocks and hurried to join the killing. He got only halfway down the slope. Judson Driscoll reached out of the shadows and wrestled the boy to the earth.

"Don't!" Willie yelled, firing a rifle shot toward Driscoll. Driscoll returned fire, and Willie felt his left foot explode.

"Here, shoot again, why don't you?" Driscoll shouted, as he raised a stricken Albert Mills as a sort of frail shield. The boy shook with terror, and Willie dragged himself to the cover of a nearby boulder.

"He's just a boy," Willie argued.

"My brother wasn't much bigger!" Driscoll countered. "Here, Mills, look here!"

Driscoll now turned the youngster toward the melee below. Mills was too busy to notice, but not so Thurman Livingston. The sheriff turned, grinning, and fired two bullets up the slope. The first nicked Jud Driscoll's shoulder, and the would-be avenger spun and fell. The second clipped Albert's ear and sent him shrieking down the hillside toward his father.

Amid the shouting and confusion, it was impossible to tell whose bullet found Albert next. One shattered a kneecap. Another carried away two fingers. As for the third and fourth and fifth, they struck together near the youngster's middle, leaving him to bleed out his life five feet from the spring.

"Lord help us all," Willie prayed, as he struggled toward the dying boy. It wasn't love for Albert that drove him on. No, it was the recollection of other Alberts, poor blind fools who had rushed into battle never dreaming of the reality of cold cruel death that awaited them.

Willie never made it. Exertion and loss of blood overcame desperation, and he sprawled in the rocks a stone's throw shy of Albert Mills.

Dewey and Joe found him when the smoke of burning shelters and discharged weapons had finally lifted from the nightmare scene.

"Major, you done it proper this time," Joe said, as he bound the wound.

"What happened?" Willie cried, as he stared at the limp bodies littering the ground beyond.

"Was a trick," Joe mumbled. "Mills was trailin' us from the time we passed the box canyon."

"They were waitin' when we went to get our horses," Dewey said, frowning. "They said we'd warn the Ruckers. Me, I aimed to kill 'em all! Only never the children. Or the women. Couldn't guess they were here."

"How many?" Willie asked.

"Dead?" Dewey asked. "Two women. Three, maybe four kids. One couldn't be older'n little Annie. Men? I counted three of them. Four of Mills' cowboys. And Albert."

"Mills?" Willie asked.

"He's gone crazy," Joe observed. "Grabbed a couple o' young ones, threatenin' to hang 'em if Rucker don't hand himself over."

"He'll do it," Willie said, closing his eyes as if to erase the notion.

"Mills will," Dewey muttered. "Not Rucker."

"I know," Willie agreed. "I know."

CHAPTER 15

By the time Joe Eagle and Dewey Hamer had escorted Willie back to Salt Fork Crossing, his foot was swollen and throbbing. Willie didn't remember much of the ride or the evening that followed. He did recall Ellen's worried greeting, and a less than sympathetic bit of doctoring.

"This is getting to be a habit," she'd remarked, after cutting the bullet out of Willie's foot. "Seems to me you ought to get wiser as you get older."

He hadn't replied. The aftereffects of chloroform had mixed with pain and blood loss to leave him dazed.

He slept most of the next day. Only toward dusk did he try to rise, and Billy immediately restrained him.

"Mama said you weren't to walk just yet," the boy explained.

"I've got things to see to," Willie argued.

"Joe's tending the horses, and Mama's seen to everything else. My job's watching you."

"Jailer, eh?"

"Could be," Billy said with a grin. "Going to make my job tough, Uncle Wil?"

"No, I'll serve out my sentence peaceable."

Ellen soon arrived with some broth, but he managed to

128

get only a little down. He had no appetite, and his stomach felt as if it were tied in knots.

Next morning, however, he was better. Using a crutch Joe had carved from a willow limb, Willie hobbled to the table and joined the Trents for breakfast. He gazed in dismay at platters of ham and eggs, though. Ellen brought a bowl of milk and offered some biscuits.

"It's the shock," she explained, as he dipped a biscuit in the milk and chewed its soggy end. "Be a time before your stomach's right again."

"Sure," Willie agreed. "I do hope it isn't a long time."

"Bet you do," Cobb said, laughing. "Milk and biscuits? Ugh!"

Willie did improve. His head cleared, anyway. The foot continued to ache, and Ellen drained it daily.

"We might ought to get you to a regular doc," Dewey suggested, when he noted the bluish tint of the skin.

"Ellie's had plenty of practice cutting bullets out of people," Willie argued. "Most of the docs out this way haven't seen half what Ellie witnessed the first week she was in Wichita, not to mention the hard times since. She was married to a doctor, wasn't she? You pick up things by and by. I remember how it was in Virginia. The regimental surgeon'd just chop off a foot and be done with it."

"Well, if they go to cuttin' off your leg, Major, I'll carve you a nice new one out o' that willow," Joe promised.

"Be Uncle Peg Leg then," Cobb declared, and his brothers cackled. Only little Annie remained mute. She walked over and wrapped an arm around Willie's legs.

"You'll get better," the girl whispered. "Mama and I prayed for you."

And whether it was the prayer or the rest that did it, Willie's foot slowly began to mend. It was a good thing, for trouble wasn't long in coming.

First, Joe Eagle spied strangers riding along the river.

"Mills' hands?" Willie whispered, when the Cheyenne shared the news.

"I'd guess 'em to be from Rucker's camp," Joe replied. "Awful young, most of 'em."

Then Mills himself appeared, together with Sheriff Livingston and a half-dozen heavily armed cowboys. With them were Warren Rucker and a boy of twelve or so.

"What's going on here?" Ellen demanded, as she charged out the front door. "And why have you got that child bound head to toe?"

Willie followed her accusing finger to the younger of the captives. Not only were his wrists securely tied but a noose hung loosely around his neck.

"He's done nothin'!!" Warren shouted, shaking with rage. "Hang me if you will, but Levi there's just twelve. He ain't done a thing to you."

"He's a Rucker," Mills said, sneering at the boy. "That's enough to merit a hanging."

"Stretch 'em both, Mr. Mills," one of the hands suggested. "Them Ruckers had time enough."

"Three days," Livingston mused. "Time aplenty."

Willie took a deep breath and leaned on his crutch. Why was it the fight always seemed to find him?

"Uncle Wil?" an anxious Billy asked, as he blocked the path to the door.

"Best I speak with 'em," Willie explained.

"I heard all about what happened at the mesa," Billy continued. "Remember Rod Hays talking about his papa, too, before he went off on the stage. I lost my papa. You won't go, too, will you?"

"I'm not so easy to kill," Willie assured the youngster. After resting a hand on Billy's head, Willie crutched his way to the door and hobbled along outside. By then Joe Eagle was at Ellen's side.

"I sent a man to Rucker three days ago," Mills was explaining to Ellen when Willie arrived. "Warned him to

130

give himself over to Thurm for trial or suffer the consequences.''

"What would those be?" Ellen asked.

"I had his boy," Mills explained, nodding toward young Levi. "His answer was to send that older boy by night, try to fetch the little one home."

"Uncle Riley didn't send me," Warren insisted. "I was trailin' you boys from the mesa, aimin' to bring Levi on home. The fight's gone out o' us, mister. We got kin to bury back home. That's why you ain't heard anything. Riley's left."

"A trick," Livingston argued.

"You should believe it," Willie said, leaning on his crutch and fighting back a wave of pain. "Let the boys go. Be an offer of peace. Might put this fighting to an end."

"Give it a chance," Ellen added. "Hasn't there been enough killing here?"

"Rucker's three days'll be up come dusk," Mills added, unaffected by the arguments. "He doesn't arrive by then, I'll hang those two down at the crossing."

"Not here!" Ellen cried. "Anywhere but here!"

"Right here," Mills added with a snarl. "Just like I promised. I'll leave them hanging there for anyone who passes by to see. It will be a reminder that I keep my promises."

"I've got children here!" Ellen shouted.

"Let them learn from others' errors," Mills went on to say. "Let it be a testimony to the fate awaiting outlaws."

"Outlaws?" Willie asked. "That boy look the part?"

"He was there, in the camp with the others," Mills said angrily. "He's close to as old as Albert was."

"And whose fault was that?" Willie countered. "I told you that boy ought not to go. You sent him with me as a spy, and you left him to die while you charged a camp full of women and babies. You keep up with this insanity, hang those boys, and Riley will be along all right. Only he won't just ransom those little ones of yours, Mills. He'll shoot them dead and come for you as well."

"Just threats," Livingston said, laughing. "Want me to pick out a tree, Mr. Mills?"

"Might as well," Mills said, gazing westward at a setting sun.

Livingston turned and rode along the river. Finally he spotted a tall oak with a branch overhanging the river. The sheriff tossed a rope over the branch and worked it until it rested in a crook eight feet over the shallows of the river. Livingston then secured one free end of rope to the trunk of the tree and formed the other into a noose.

"Looks like your pa don't have much use for you, boy!" the sheriff said as he rode, grinning, past Levi Rucker.

"He's got Ma to look after," Levi said, mustering his courage.

"Could be they're tellin' the truth, you know," Livingston noted. "Nobody's seen hide nor tail o' them raiders."

"So they'd like us to believe," Mills answered.

"There's a way to hedge your bet, though," Livingston suggested. "Hang one today. Hold the other a bit."

"Clever idea," Mills agreed, eyeing the two captives.

"You hang Levi, Uncle Riley won't much bother about me," Warren growled. "He'll cut your heart out. If you be bound and determined to do it, then I'm the one."

"Be better payment for Albert to choose the younger one," Mills said, nudging his horse in the direction of the twelve-year-old. Levi paled, and his lip quivered as he searched for words. Somehow the boy looked thinner. His dark hair fell over his forehead in a haphazard manner, and his patched trousers and homespun shirt were a stark contrast to Abner Mills's tailored suit and silk cuffs.

"You go and do it!" Levi said, ducking Mills's touch. "But know Pa'll burn more'n a town next time."

"Feisty little scamp, isn't he?" Mills asked, jerking on the loose end of the noose hanging around Levi's neck. The boy lurched sideways, tumbled to the ground, and landed in a heap beside his horse.

"That's enough!" Willie shouted, but he was unable to

move fast enough to prevent Mills from producing a raw-hide whip and adding to the boy's torment. Joe Eagle, on the other hand, flew across the dusty ground and tore Mills from his horse. It was the rancher's turn to tumble earthward.

"Thurm!" Mills yelled, as the Cheyenne tore the whip from Mills's grip and began thrashing the rancher merci-lessly. A pair of cowboys tried their best to pry Joe from their boss, but rage lent its strength to Joe's blows and he wouldn't be dislodged. Sheriff Livingston finally rode over and clubbed Joe across the head with a rifle barrel. The Cheyenne collapsed.

"Use your second rope on him!" Mills shouted angrily, as he arose, battered and bleeding.

"I wouldn't!" Willie warned, as he drew a pistol.

"Now, you don't mean to interfere, do you?" Mills asked.

"I guess it's my turn," Willie said, collecting his strength. "Ellie, help Joe inside."

"You've picked the wrong side, Fletcher!" Mills warned.

"It's happened before," Willie replied.

Ellen tried to raise Joe from the ground, but he was too much for her. Dewey and Billy raced out of the house, though, and each took a leg. Ellen cradled the unconscious Indian's shoulders, and the three of them managed to get Joe into the house.

"Always figured it would come down to this," Livingston said, dismounting. "I recognize you from Kansas."

"That's your bad luck," Willie said, glaring at the lawman.

"Willie, no!" Ellen called from the door.

"They've drawn the line," Willie told her. "It's my fight now."

"Why?" Mills asked, as he recovered his wits. "Because of that Indian? He only got what he earned. Or is it these young outlaws here?"

"I never in my life stomached a hanging like this," Willie answered. "You self-righteous fools think you can twist the law to suit your personal whims!"

"They burned a town," Livingston pointed out. "Killed two people."

"And how many did you kill at the river? How many on Blood Mesa?" Willie shouted.

"Many a man's paid for that business at the river," Livingston said, stepping away from his horse. "A man who'd hunt down cowboys one by one won't be put off by the killin' of a few women and kids. Maybe he's gone home, and maybe not. Either way, he'll be back here sooner or later to finish what he started."

"He will if you hang those boys," Willie declared. "Let them go. He'll deem it a favor and consider he owes you. That's how he is. I know him."

"It's a notion, boss," Livingston said.

"A poor one," Mills answered. "A man never bargains from weakness. No, I'll compromise. Hang the older one, Thurm. We'll save the minnow for later."

"No!" Levi screamed, struggling to gain his feet. Two cowboys wrestled the boy onto his horse and held him there. Livingston led Warren's horse out to the river, exchanged the harmless noose for the deadly one attached to the tree, and prepared to whip the horse into motion.

"You can't do this," Willie said, hobbling on. He couldn't control his pistol and manage the crutch at the same time, however, and a cowboy managed to circle around and knock the pistol from his hand.

"You don't appear to be in a position to stop us anymore, Fletcher," Mills noted.

"We are!" Ellen yelled, pointing a rifle out of the back window. Dewey, too, held a Winchester, and for a moment Mills hesitated.

"Before I rode onto Blood Mesa, I had never harmed a woman," Mills said, staring hard at the house. "I'm afraid I wouldn't hesitate to do so again. You might get off a few shots, Mrs. Trent. Maybe you could even kill me. I assure you, however, my men would offer you and your boys a most unpleasant fate.''

''Was his people killed Uncle Rupe,'' Dewey said, swallowing hard. ''I hold it against 'em plenty, but this here's just murder!''

''If you're sure of your facts, hold a trial in Throckmorton, Sheriff,'' Ellen suggested.

''No, we'll just get some extra ropes ready,'' Mills growled.

''Don't do it, ma'am,'' Warren pleaded, as he felt the sheriff tighten the noose against his throat. ''There's been dyin' enough hereabouts. Do what you can for my little cousin Levi.''

''You can't hang him!'' Willie cried.

''Oh, I can,'' Mills insisted. ''I will, in fact.''

''You spoke up for me, too, Major,'' Warren called. ''I thank you for it. Don't figure anything's to be done now, though. My horse's skittish, and he'll run if a shot's fired. Don't leave me in much shape to see sunrise.''

''I won't let you do this,'' Willie said, struggling toward the river. A rider turned his horse, knocking Willie sideways. He landed in a nest of prickly pear, and his ankle exploded in pain. A mixture of agony and pure fury boiled up inside him, and he screamed so that the air itself seemed to split in two.

Thurman Livingston slapped Warren's horse a second later, and the animal raced toward the riverbank, leaving its rider to slowly choke beneath the oak limb.

''It's done,'' Mills announced minutes later, laughing as he turned Levi's head toward the dangling corpse of his cousin. ''Your turn's next.''

''I ain't scairt,'' Levi said hatefully. ''Word o' this'll bring Pa back here. He's got his view o' justice, too.''

''Justice!'' Mills shouted. ''Hear the pup, Thurm? Justice? That's justice there, hanging from yon tree.''

''No, that's just death,'' Willie said, as he rolled free of the cactus. "Once you get it started, there's no stopping it, either."

"Meaning?" Livingston said, swinging a rifle toward Willie's chest.

"Bide your time, Livingston," Willie warned. "You don't have much of it left to you."

Mills and his men rode off then. Dewey emerged from the house a few moments later to help Willie back inside.

"Joe?" Willie asked.

"He'll be all right," Dewey assured him. "Miz Trent's lookin' after him."

"Cut down that boy," Willie pleaded.

"I'll do it," Dewey pledged. "He might've been the very one that kilt Uncle Rupe, but I wouldn't wish this on him."

"Nor'd I," Willie agreed, as he sat on the porch steps.

Even as Dewey headed for the hanging tree, the sun began to dip below the western horizon. In the faint scarlet glow of dusk the land itself seemed suddenly bathed in red—bloodred.

An owl hooted eerily down in the river bottom, and Willie scowled. It was an old omen of death, the owl's voice.

"You're a mite late," he whispered to the bird.

Then he gazed out at the river and saw Warren's limp frame reflected in the Salt Fork. Death matched death. "An eye for an eye," the Bible read. Riley Rucker trusted in such words.

Boy was right, Willie thought. He'll be back.

CHAPTER 16

Willie sat in a corner of the front room that night, sipping broth and watching the flames dance across the logs in the fireplace.

"Your foot still hurting, Uncle Wil?" Cobb asked, as he settled in beside Willie.

"Some," Willie confessed. It wasn't pain that had darkened his brow, though. It was knowing the world had again gone mad, that a nightmare had descended on Throckmorton County.

"We've weathered hard times before," Ellen had said at supper. "We'll do so again."

But Willie wondered how many times he could dodge fate when death seemed so close at hand. And in a world of Thurman Livingstons and Abner Millses—men who would drop a noose over a boy's head—was it possible to avoid catastrophe?

Willie wasn't the only one haunted by that evening's events. Dewey Hamer was changed. The young man had seemingly vanished when Mills and Livingston first arrived. Now he stood sullenly by a window, gazing outside into the darkness as if some unknown terror lurked there.

As for Joe Eagle, the Cheyenne rested quietly on a pile of

quilts in the back room. His head was wrapped in bandages, and his blue-black jaw and forehead attested to the sheriff's hard blow.

"Best thing for him's rest," Ellen had explained when the boys begged to visit. Now little Annie stood like a guard in front of the door.

"I'm Joe's nurse," she proclaimed. "Leave him be, Mama says."

"Will Joe be all right?" Willie asked Ellen later, after the boys had crawled into their blankets beside the fire.

"Seems to me you ought to be concerned about your foot," she answered. "That fool stunt of yours started the bleeding again, and the last thing I needed was to pluck cactus spines out of your leathery hide."

"Couldn't help myself," he told her. "Had to try and stop it."

"You couldn't stop anything," she said, turning away to rub a tear from her eyes. "You never could. And me? One word from Abner Mills and I surrender."

"How's Joe?" Willie asked, shifting the subject.

"He's likely suffering a concussion, but he'll be all right," she answered. "Came to an hour ago, long enough to smile at Annie. They're close, those two."

"I feel like this is all my fault," he muttered.

"It isn't," she objected. "You can't help what happens. And you can't blame yourself for all the evil that visits life."

"Can't I?"

"You shouldn't," she said, intertwining the fingers of her left hand with his. "It's the world we live in. Too much anger and greed. Too many men like Abner Mills."

"And Riley?"

"I can almost understand him," she said, sighing. "But Mills, well, he's a puzzle. Why come here in the first place? And what could have brought him to take little Albert to Blood Mesa, knowing as he did what was sure to happen?"

"I've asked myself that once or twice," Willie confessed.

"Ask yourself something else," she whispered. "What was he doing while Riley held the children captive at the school?"

"Hiding," Willie muttered.

"You think Riley let those youngsters go out of gratitude to you for some wartime debt? Well I haven't noticed that side of him, myself. No, Willie, he felt sorry for those children. He didn't want my youngsters on his conscience, and he couldn't bring himself to murder the Mills boys or Alice, knowing as he did by then that their father wouldn't raise a hand to stop it."

"I wouldn't count too heavily on that, Ellie."

"Not anymore," she agreed grimly. "Not after tonight."

Willie nodded his agreement. And shortly thereafter he lay down on a blanket, feeling the cold, hard floor underneath. The fire provided the room with a hair of warmth, though, and the dozing youngsters nearby chased the chill usually brought on by nightfall. At least there were others to share the terror.

Willie awoke a few minutes shy of midnight. There were horses splashing across the river, and he hurried to pull on his clothes. By then Dewey was at the door, Winchester in hand, and Ellen was taking her shotgun down from its perch above the door.

"Who is it?" Cobb mumbled, as he sat up in bed.

"The hangman's come back!" Annie screamed.

"Rest easy," Willie said, wincing as he tried to stand. "I'll have a look."

"It's for me to do," Dewey argued.

Before either could step outside, though, a loud voice rang out across the crossing.

"I come to settle accounts!" Riley Rucker barked. "Come on out o' there 'fore I have to torch the place!"

"There's nobody here you want!" Ellen screamed in answer.

"Come out and let me see for myself!" Riley ordered.

"Come in if you've the nerve!" Dewey challenged.

"Hush!" Willie said, grabbing his crutch and hobbling toward the door. "Riley, it's me, Willie. The ones you're after are elsewhere."

"I'm done trustin' others," Riley replied.

"Me?" Willie asked.

"Anybody," Riley explained, sliding off his horse. A pair of men lit torches, and the bearded riders gazed with hate-filled eyes at the drowsy faces peering out the door and windows.

"It's Mills you want," Willie said, crutching his way onto the porch. "Unless you've taken to murdering children."

"Don't talk to me of children!" Riley stormed. "I buried a boy of my own yesterday! Now it's time to bury others!"

"Not here," Willie said, holding out his open palms. "Your fight's not with me. Nor with these others."

"My fight's with the whole world, it seems," Riley insisted. "Lord, Major, I laid Rachel to rest back home. Put my youngest, Aaron, at her side. He was seven. Seven! No bigger'n a cricket, Willie, and those snakes shot him down with no more regard than a farmer'd have for a fox in his chicken coop."

"I know," Willie said sourly. "I was up there myself."

"Saw you," Riley said, studying Willie with cool rage. "It's why I come."

"You didn't need to burn the town," Willie said, blinking away the vision of Esperanza's dying anguish. "Or to kill those men in the hotel."

"Things got out of hand there," Riley explained. "Fool of a clerk fired on my outfit. Boys shot back. Stableman and the storekeeper got caught in the middle."

"Somebody's always caught in the middle," Willie grumbled.

"Guess it's you this time, huh?"

"Appears so, Riley."

"You shot Jud Driscoll up on the mountain, Willie,"

Riley said, stepping closer. "And Lem Cranmers back in town."

"I did," Willie confessed. "First time to save a friend. The second to save myself."

"You and that Indian tracked us for Mills."

"We did, Riley, in hopes of treating with you. Mills played us false, and he rode down on your camp. I'm sorry for that. He paid with the life of his eldest boy."

"Heard that," Riley muttered. "My eldest, Levi, has got off somewhere. Sent Warren to find him, but neither one's turned up. It'd go far toward payin' for Rachel and Aaron if you could steer me toward those boys."

"Warren's down by the river," Dewey announced, joining Willie on the porch. The sixteen-year-old stood ready with his rifle, but Riley didn't react to the weapon.

"There's a grave there, Riley," a youngish rider observed.

"I buried him," Dewey explained.

"Kill him?" Riley asked, his face reddening.

"No," Dewey answered. "Might have if I'd caught him at the river or such. Was my uncle you shot at the hotel. But as it happened, Abner Mills hung Warren."

"Hung?" a pair of riders cried.

"With your blessin'?" Riley gasped.

"He did what he could to stop it," Dewey declared. "Poor Joe Eagle got himself clubbed silly. Me, I just watched. It wasn't somethin' I'll be forgettin' anytime soon."

"Mills said he sent word he'd trade Warren for you," Willie said, trying to step between Dewey and the angry riders. "Three days he waited. So he hung Warren."

"I see," Riley grunted. "Never got his message. Was up buryin' Rachel and the boy. Then I got my girl Leanna and her two little brothers down to Granbury where they'll be safe with my sister Jeannie. Took Jubal's three there, too. All that's left of the family, I suppose, now Warren's gone. Nothin' o' Ray left."

"Memories," Willie said, shivering as the wind blew harsh and cold off the river.

"Memories don't breed sons," Riley said, shaking with fury. "You're not tellin' it all, Major. What is it you've left out?"

"Nothin'!" Dewey insisted.

"I told you Levi's gotten off somewhere," Riley said, fuming. "You've seen him, haven't you? Where is he?"

"Mills has him," Willie said, avoiding Riley's fiery stare.

"He was fixin' to hang him, too," Dewey added, "only Wil argued him out of it."

"How long'll he wait?" Riley asked. " 'Fore he hangs my boy."

"I don't know," Willie confessed.

"He says he'll trade the boy for you," Ellen called from the door.

"He won't," Willie declared, frowning. "Riley, the dead are buried. Why not head down to your sister's place while you still can?"

"That time's long past."

"You stay, and more people are certain to die."

"The right ones this time!"

"Right ones? Is there any such thing?"

"They got Levi!" Riley shouted. "I helped birth that boy. I rocked him on my knee, taught him to ride, mended his tears and splinted his breaks. It's my blood flows through him!"

"I don't know where he is," Willie said, "but I'll find him."

"Willie!" Ellen warned.

"You got fine intentions, Willie, and you've known some hard fights. You never read men worth a hoot, though," Riley declared. "There's a stone where this Mills ought to have a heart. He don't care for his own young, and he'd murder mine. If Levi's still alive, it's only me can bring him back."

"How so?" Willie asked.

"By killin' Mills. Burnin' him out o' his house, if that's what it takes. Makin' him so scairt he won't dare harm my boy."

"He's not the kind to scare," Willie argued. "Give me tomorrow to find the boy, to get him back here."

"Aim to set a trap for me, Major?"

"Wait nearby," Willie suggested. "Have somebody watch the crossing. Once I've got Levi, I'll bring him to you. You can see I won't allow myself to be followed."

"It's a fool's play, Willie," Riley observed. "You won't make any friends for doin' it."

"Wasn't friends I was seeking," Willie answered.

"You can't," Ellen argued. "Your foot's—"

"I can ride," Willie assured her. "Well enough to do what's required."

"You ain't changed much," Riley said, shaking his head. "I recall Ray sayin' you used to read stories out of some fool book about knights and sword fights and castles."

"King Arthur," Willie said, smiling as he recalled it. The book was lost outside Fredericksburg in '63.

"I'll wait till nightfall tomorrow," Riley promised. "No longer."

"That's time enough to bring the boy to you," Willie said.

"Breathin' or not," Riley said, choking with emotion. "It's a fool's play, like I say, Willie, but Lord help you, I hope you manage it."

"And if I do, you'll go home?"

"Seems a fair price to pay for Levi," Riley said, dropping his eyes. "If Mills hurts that boy, though, God have mercy. I won't."

Willie nodded his understanding.

After the Rucker band had left, Willie tried to find some rest. Little came. He stirred at dawn, weary but hopeful. Billy saddled the gray, and Ellen packed food for the journey.

143

"Won't anybody thank you," Dewey argued as he followed Willie outside. "Just look at you! You can barely walk. That foot's hurtin', too."

"I got something to do, Dewey," Willie explained. "Maybe it's like Riley says, a fool's play. But I can't get the look of that boy out of my dreams. I got to try."

"You don't," Dewey complained.

"Sure I do," Willie declared. "And maybe if I get Levi back to his papa, Riley'll keep his word and skedaddle."

"That won't stop Mills."

"Then I will," Willie muttered. "May have to, just to pry Levi loose."

"Most likely they've already kilt that boy," Dewey said, sighing. "But there's a chance. I'll admit that. Only you can't manage it alone."

"I've done harder things."

"Maybe, but not with one leg," Dewey observed. "Joe's only half-alive. Guess it's up to me to go."

"You don't have to," Willie said. "Your heart's not in it."

"Sure it is," Dewey said, heading for his horse. "Just spare me a few minutes to saddle my paint. I can be as big a fool as you."

"Appears so," Willie noted.

And moments later the two of them were setting out from Salt Fork Crossing on their fool's errand.

Lord, help us, Willie prayed silently. Let me bring that boy back safe and end this nightmare.

CHAPTER 17

There had been so many horses trampling the sandy soil along the Salt Fork of the Brazos that past week that at first Willie had difficulty sifting through the trails. One led north and another south. Others headed east and west.

"They wouldn't cross the river," Dewey pointed out, "and they sure wouldn't ride toward the mesa. Esperanza? Maybe. Most likely they'd circle around south toward the Mills place and wait for Rucker to send word."

"You're learning," Willie noted.

"Could be," Dewey agreed. "Why wouldn't he just ride straight to his ranch?"

"He may be a hard man, but I don't figure Mrs. Mills to take easy her husband bringing a child in with a noose hanging around his neck."

"There's other folks there who'd argue it, too," Dewey said, frowning. "So he'll pass some time elsewhere first. The Ruckers know about Granny Gunnerson's place, but Uncle Sime's farm down south's another story."

"Not an easy place to sneak up on, either," Willie observed. "Let's try it, Dewey."

The young man turned his paint and led the way. Willie, in turn, picked his way along the rocky trail toward the farm formerly owned by Simon Hamer. Halfway there Willie spotted a swath cut in the high yellow grass to his left. Riding out that way, he found bits of cloth caught on pencil cactus spines.

"Over here, Dewey," Willie called, and his partner turned back.

Willie traced a path across the rocky ground. Other bits of torn flannel—red-and-black plaid—were caught on briers or cactus spines. In one sandy stretch the earth was scraped and torn.

"Look there," Dewey said, pointing to a strip of plaid cloth. It was bloody, and there were droplets of blood elsewhere nearby.

"You've got sharp eyes," Willie said, shuddering as he located a shoe behind a nearby rock.

"Somethin's been drug through here, Major," Dewey declared.

"His heart couldn't be that cold!" Willie said, fighting the realization.

"Got to be," Dewey insisted, as he rode on ahead. There was more blood, and skin scrapings besides. Another shoe lay in the trail, and clumps of hair were caught in another nest of briers.

"Not something," Willie finally admitted. "Someone."

"They drug that poor boy through here," Dewey said, growing alternately pale with shock and red with fury.

Willie turned southwest with the blood trail and started up the slope of a hill overlooking the river. Halfway up he noticed an unusual clump to his right. He nudged the gray in that direction, then froze. There, battered and bruised, torn by thorns and scraped raw by ground, lay the nearly naked body of Levi Rucker.

"Lord help us," Willie muttered, as he swung down from his saddle and gingerly stepped closer. Hard as it was to believe, the boy was still breathing.

"Pa?" Levi called, reaching his bloody hands toward Willie.

"Not your pa, but a friend all the same," Willie said, cradling the youngster's head.

"I never told 'em where our camp was, Pa," Levi said, sobbing. "No matter what they did."

"It's all right," Willie said, pulling a canteen off his horse and offering Levi a drink. "You'll be all right."

"Pa?" the boy asked, as Willie wet a kerchief and washed the blood and grit from the youngster's forehead. Levi opened his eyes wider and blinked rapidly. "Pa?"

"It's Willie Delamer," Willie whispered. "I met you a time back at your place up north."

"Huh?"

"Served with your papa in the war against the North."

"Where's Pa?"

"Safe," Willie assured the boy. "I'll get you to him."

"Best hurry," a hitherto unheard voice spoke. Willie gazed up at two Mills hands who had been watching from the crest of the hill.

"He ain't got much livin' left to him," the second cowboy added, laughing. "We burned off just about all there was of him but raw meat. Thought he was dead. You did us a service, comin' along as you did. We were leavin'."

Levi's eyes finally managed to focus, and he shuddered at the sight of the two cowboys.

"Dewey?" Willie called, but young Hamer seemed to have vanished from the earth.

"Now that's funny," the first cowboy said, scratching his head. "I swear there was another one down the hill. Where's he gotten to?"

"Never you mind," the second one said. "We'll finish this pair and then worry about him. You want first shot?"

"Why waste a bullet?" his companion asked, pulling a knife from his boot. He stepped toward Levi, but Willie leaped out and knocked the would-be murderer aside. In the process Willie landed hard on his bad foot, and the pain brought him to his knees.

"No!" Willie shouted, as he saw the second cowboy

approach Levi. Then two rifles barked, and both of the hirelings spun and fell.

"Dewey?" Willie called.

"He's well enough, Major," Riley Rucker called, as he climbed the hill toward his son. "Knew you two'd track 'em for us. Now I'd judge it's for me to look after my boy."

"Pa!" Levi cried, and Riley knelt beside the boy and drew him close.

"What sort of devil could manage such a thing?" Riley asked, as he examined the youngster's battered body. "Can I trouble you for that canteen, Major?"

"Here," Willie said, offering it to his old comrade. "It's not far to the crossing. Ellen Trent's no doctor, but she's got a way with healing, and she's a wonder with children."

"I heard about her," Riley said, as he bathed his son's heaving chest. Levi's breathing was labored, and convulsions wracked his body.

"Wrap this around him," Dewey suggested, when he finally appeared. Riley accepted a wool blanket and covered Levi's shivering body. Already the boy's eyes were growing faint, however. His fingers were no longer able to grip his father's hand.

"Pa?" he murmured.

"I'm here, Levi," Riley answered. "Right here beside you."

"Guess I'll be seein' Ma sooner'n we figured," the boy said. Just for a moment the glassy film left his eyes, and Levi lifted his head. "You'll take me home, won't you?"

"Sure I will, son."

"Then it won't be so bad. It don't hurt now, Pa. Pa?"

"Yes, son," Riley said, bending low over the boy's mouth. Levi's hands went limp then, and his head dropped back against the bloody ground.

"Dear Lord," Willie said, turning away.

"That's a fine notion, Major," Riley said, easing the blanket around Levi's frail form. "Pray hard. You especially pray for the one that did this. He'll need God's help, as I do aim to afflict him mightily!''

"Riley . . ." Willie began, trying to offer comfort. But the distraught father would have none of it.

"Look at him, Major!" Riley screamed. "Peeled raw, and fightin' 'em all the time. Nobody ought to have to die that way!"

"At least he wasn't alone," Willie declared.

"I thank you for that, Willie. You and me, we've buried boys before. How many were there in Virginia like this? Not a man-hair to 'em, but they rode a true soldier's trail."

"I don't recall numbers," Willie said, limping toward his horse. "Too many. It tears my heart to add another to the ranks. It's time this was ended, though."

"Ended?" Riley screamed. "It's only beginnin'."

"No, Riley," a grizzled rider argued. "Road's grown long. It's time to go home and see to things."

"Enough have perished," a second added. "Let's get Levi along home."

Riley shook with fury, but the others dismounted and took charge of him. They tied Levi atop a spare horse and then got Riley on his mount. Finally they turned and rode northward in silence, leaving the bloody hillside to Willie and Dewey Hamer.

"Is this the end of it?" Dewey whispered.

"Maybe," Willie said, staring first at the bloodstained ground and later at the two corpses nearby. "If not, the end'll come pretty soon."

"Sure," Dewey agreed. "One way or the other."

They returned to Salt Fork Crossing in silence.

"Did you find the boy?" Ellen asked when they returned.

Willie nodded somberly. The questions on her lips, however, died when she noticed the despair painted on his face.

"I only rode in to see how Joe was coming along,"

149

Willie explained when he dismounted. "Figure it's time I was back at the cabin, tending my horses."

"Well, that's nonsense," she said, pointing to his foot. Blood had seeped through the cloth bindings, and Willie couldn't hide the resulting pain from his face.

"I'll see to the gray," Dewey said, taking charge of the horses. "Best you get that foot tended to."

Ellen handed him his crutch, and he hobbled to the house unaided. Once inside, Billy and Cobb rushed to help him to the kitchen, where Ellen cut away the bandages and re-dressed his wound.

"There'll be no arguing about this, Willie," she scolded. "You're to pass the next week here, where there are people to attend you. I want that foot idle, and that's an order."

"Yes, ma'am," Willie said, managing half a smile.

"You could use the rest, and I could stand the company," she added. "As for Joe, he's improved. He managed to keep a slice of ham down this afternoon, and his eyes are less blurred."

"He mends fast," Willie noted.

"I won't have him pushed, either," she chided. "Now, what would you say to slicing some potatoes? I've got a turkey baking, and—"

"A turkey?" Willie asked, surprised.

"I shot it, Uncle Wil," Billy boasted. "Usin' Joe's rifle."

"Good for you," Willie said, patting the boy's back. "You're growing every day, son. Eleventh birthday isn't far away."

"No," Billy said, stepping close and burrowing his head into Willie's side. "Be the first one without Papa."

"Sure," Willie muttered.

"You'll be here, won't you?"

"Of course," Ellen said nervously. "Won't you, Willie?"

"Hard to guess what the future'll bring," Willie answered. He gazed out the window, and his mind wandered. Billy settled in on one knee.

"They killed Levi Rucker, didn't they?" Billy whispered after Ellen left the room.

"What?" Willie asked, blinking himself back to reality.

"I was asking about Levi," Billy explained.

"Oh," Willie said, sighing. "Lord, would you look at me? I'm sitting here rocking you like a babe, and here you've gone and shot us supper."

"It's all right," Billy remarked. "Felt sort of good. Papa used to do it."

"You're too old for such foolishness now," Willie said, letting the youngster slide off onto a nearby bench. "It's a shame, I sometimes think, how boys grow themselves up so fast. Always in a hurry to shave, my papa used to say."

"I haven't got any whiskers," Billy mumbled.

"You got some time to grow 'em." Unlike some, Willie thought.

"Uncle Wil, you figure it's hard, dying young?"

"I never done it," Willie answered, nervously avoiding Billy's probing eyes.

"Was it hard for Levi?"

"I never said—"

"You didn't have to," Billy said, frowning. "Shoot, I knew he was killed when I saw your eyes. Wasn't hung, was he?"

"No," Willie assured the boy.

"Good," Billy whispered. "Cobb and Ellis've had some nightmares lately about hanging."

"Oh?"

"Last night. You, too, I think."

"Weighs heavy on a soul, such things," Willie explained. "Hard to figure the way the world's turned crazy. A good man like your papa is shot. Whole town's burned to the ground! Boys who ought to be busy with chores and school lessons get buried instead."

"But it's over now, Mama says."

"I hope so," Willie said, pulling the boy close. "Pray so."

"I pray a lot these days," Billy confessed. "Cobb and Ellis, too. Even Annie."

"Never hurts," Willie observed.

"Know what for, Uncle Wil?" Willie shook his head, and Billy took a deep breath. "We pray you'll stick close by."

"Kind of hope for that myself," Willie admitted.

"Then maybe this time our praying'll get an answer."

"Maybe so," Willie said, as he lifted the boy's chin.

Later that afternoon while slicing potatoes, Willie found himself alone with Ellen. She, too, asked about Levi Rucker. He didn't answer her question, but his eyes again betrayed the truth.

"Maybe you were right to suggest we leave this place," she said, as she dropped a slab of lard into her skillet. "It does seem to be a place of death."

"You'd have company down on the Clear Fork," Willie noted. "Irene would be handy, and Elvira Slocum'd be just up the road."

"Irene's close to a sister, being married to Trav," she remarked. "I don't know her all that well, but she seems a fine person."

"Better'n the one I got for a sister-in-law," Willie grumbled. "But then Trav's a step above what calls himself my brother."

"You could run your horses down there?"

"Better water," Willie declared. "I'm sure I can sell off the acreage up here. Mills would buy this place off you."

"And you would breed horses?"

"It's a notion. I had a start toward a ranch up north, on the Sweetwater, only things didn't work out."

"The Indian wars, you mean."

"Always been that way. One war or another coming along."

"You could always run cattle like Trav."

"Maybe," Willie said, sadly eyeing the scene outside the window. "Trail-driving days are fading, though. They expect the railroad in Weatherford before summer. Be the end of drives to Kansas when the tracks get this far west. Easier to ship 'em in rail cars."

"Things will be more civilized," Ellen argued. "Churches and schools. Law and order."

"Like Abner Mills brought to Esperanza?" Willie asked. "No, thanks just the same."

"It hasn't been all his fault, Willie."

"Mostly, it has. Lord, Ellie, if you'd seen what he did to Levi!"

"Tell me," she implored.

"Can't," he muttered. "I don't want to think on it. If I see that boy's face again I believe I'll ride out and shoot that devil myself!"

"I suppose that's another reason for moving south to the Clear Fork."

"Might do you and the little ones good to dodge some shadows, too."

"I've faced up to my ghosts," she explained. "And I've done what I could to help the children past theirs. Truth is, I've been almost happy here. As close to it as I've been anywhere."

"Even in Kansas, when Jack was still alive?"

"Kansas was one fight after another," she said, shuddering as the recollection flooded her mind. "Those were hard, cruel times for the most part. Here, for a while, we were part of a community. We saw a town bloom in this godforsaken llano. But it's gone now, all of it."

The lard had melted down by then, and Ellen began to toss potato slices into the skillet. Soon she was busy frying, and the youngsters hurried in to watch.

"Ellis, your turn to set the table," she instructed. "Cobb, is the kindling box full? Billy, how's the water barrel stand?"

She even had Annie set out a wash basin.

Later, when the chores were completed and potatoes ready, she set the children to scrubbing hands and faces while Willie carried a platter of food to Joe Eagle.

"You ought to marry that woman," the Cheyenne argued. "She cooks just fine."

"Better'n my ma," Dewey said, poking his head through the door.

"Thin as you are, that ain't much of an argument," Joe replied.

Willie grinned as his two companions sparred with words. It was a sign Joe was mending, and a hint that Dewey would survive the nightmare morning.

That night, after stuffing themselves with turkey, corn bread dressing, and fried potatoes, the Trents gathered at the fireplace and listened to Willie narrate a tale of wintering in the Big Horns. Talk of tall mountains and frozen lakes carried them away to other, distant times.

When he'd finished, Annie rushed to tend Joe Eagle while Ellen listened to her boys' prayers. Willie and Dewey spread their blankets beside the hearth, and the little Trents huddled between the two.

"You say your prayers, Uncle Wil?" Billy whispered after his brothers were fast asleep.

"Yes I did," Willie answered.

"You ask for anything?"

"Just peace," Willie whispered. "Right now I believe that would be enough."

Billy nestled in under one arm, and Annie dragged her blankets over so as to settle in on the other side. The warmth and the belonging was enough to offer hope.

But not enough to stave off the nightmares. By midnight Willie was thrashing around, and it took Dewey to rouse him from his terrors.

"Sorry," Willie said, as his eyes opened. He shook cold sweat from his forehead and fought to drive the phantoms from his mind.

"We all get 'em sometimes," Annie said, offering a reassuring touch. "Even Joe."

"Even me," Billy confessed. "But they don't last long."

No, Willie told himself. Just a lifetime.

CHAPTER 18

Actually, the worst of the nightmares did pass. For a week after Levi Rucker's death an uneasy peace settled over Salt Fork Crossing. Willie rested, and his foot began to mend. Joe Eagle rose from his bed and regained his old energy.

The stagecoaches that sometimes stopped at the river brought news of the outside world. Dewey Hamer added tidbits he picked up riding to and from the box canyon, where he looked after the mustangs trapped there and occasionally brought one back to the corral Willie had built beside the river.

"There's not been a hint of trouble lately," Dewey explained, as he marched toward the porch one bright March afternoon. "Seems it's over, Major."

"Hope so," Willie had replied.

"You know, if it wasn't for all those burned-out buildings up in Esperanza, you'd never know there'd been a fight."

"Sure," Willie agreed. "That and the headstones."

The moment Willie spoke, he was sorry for it. The words turned Dewey sour, and even an afternoon of gentling horses didn't bring back the young man's smile.

It was almost supper time when Loretta Mills appeared

with her daughter Alice. The girl wasted no time climbing down and greeting Ellen. Loretta stayed in her carriage, holding back the urge to chastise her daughter.

"Ma'am, I don't know how good an idea it is for you to be out in this country toward dusk," Willie said, as he limped over.

"We're not alone," the woman pointed out. Aside from the thin young man driving the carriage, a pair of cowboys trailed along.

"Wise to take precautions," Willie said, thinking to himself that those three wouldn't last more than a minute in an ambush.

"At any rate," Loretta continued, "this latest unpleasantness is concluded at long last."

Unpleasantness? Willie thought. There were those who referred to the War as "unpleasantness." "Murder" would have been a more apt term.

"I truly hope so, Mrs. Mills," Ellen said, offering her guest a cup of tea.

"Thank you, no," Loretta said, declining the offer. "I've merely come on Abner's behalf to tell the neighbors he plans to begin spring roundup soon. There will be a gathering of the men Tuesday week at the south line camp."

"Uncle Sime's old place," Dewey added.

"And in the meantime," Loretta went on, "Abner's summoned a Baptist preacher from Fort Worth to bless our efforts at a Sunday gathering. Afterward we'll have a dance. I'm hoping you will attend, Mrs. Trent. There are so few children here now, and my little ones hunger for company."

"Little ones?" Dewey asked, staring at Alice. The girl was half a head taller than he was.

"We'll consider it," Ellen replied. "There's so much work to do, getting ready for planting and all. And not everyone's fully mended."

"Yes," Loretta agreed, trembling slightly as a dark thought swept over her. "Still, there will be all manner of amusement. Bring the children, won't you? There are seldom any chances for them to enjoy themselves in this barren land.''

"You'll come, won't you, Dewey?" Alice asked. "I'll save a dance for you."

"Rather dance with my horse," Dewey muttered under his breath. To Alice he merely nodded.

"Come along now, daughter," Loretta called, and Alice dutifully returned to the carriage. Moments later it rolled away, bound for the Mills Ranch down south.

"Well?" Ellen asked Willie, when the dust had settled.

"Times must be harder'n I thought," Willie remarked. "No engraved invitations!"

"We can go, can't we?" Billy asked excitedly. "Jake used to talk about the parties his papa had. Whole tables of food, and more games than even Joe could imagine."

"I've got no use for that Mills fellow," Willie growled.

"It's not Abner's party," Ellen pointed out.

"Isn't it?" Willie retorted. "Victory party, if you ask me. Have you forgotten he fired you from the school?"

"Isn't it time to forget and forgive?" she asked in turn.

"Some things can never be forgotten," Willie said, shaking his head sadly. "Nor forgiven, either."

Nevertheless, after considerable goading, Willie was persuaded to load up the wagon and drive Ellen and her brood to the Mills place that Sunday. It was a sight, the lot of them decked out in their best clothes, with string ties and brown matching jackets. Willie felt confined in the scratchy wool trousers, and he missed his gray cavalry hat.

It was almost worth the discomfort, though, to see Ellen. She wore a bright yellow dress, newly sewn to match the spring weather. Annie traipsed along at her mother's side, in like costume and wearing an even brighter smile.

Annie's escort was Joe Eagle. If Willie was out of place in his fine clothes, Joe must have imagined himself caught up in a nightmare. As it happened, Joe's tie lasted but a few

158

moments, and the jacket found the wagon bed shortly thereafter.

"I'm afraid I must have been misunderstood," Loretta Mills explained, after the Baptist minister had concluded a marathon sermon. "The invitation was extended to you and the children. And to young Mr. Hamer, naturally. I never intended that Indian—"

"Mr. Eagle is a guest in my house," Ellen interrupted. "And a friend. If he's unwelcome, I'm afraid we must all be leaving."

"Well, I never imagined such a thing!" Loretta cried, hurrying off to locate her husband. Abner Mills was busy with Sheriff Livingston, and the two cowboys Loretta sent to suggest Joe depart shied away when they took note of the knife in the Cheyenne's boot and the twin Winchesters standing ready beneath the wagon seat.

"Glad you came now?" Willie asked, as he led Ellen to the dance floor. A pair of fiddlers struck up a tune, and an accordion player joined in.

"It's been a long time," she said, sighing.

"Me, I'd rather ride a rank stallion than put up with these sneers and whispers. We've got nothing in common with these people."

"They're the closest thing to neighbors that we have," Ellen argued.

"I know some cottonmouths down at the river that make for better friends," Willie grumbled.

"Hush," she scolded, pointing to where Billy and his two brothers were shooting marbles with Jake and Jonathan Mills. "It's for the children we came," she added. "Look there at Dewey."

Willie was long past considering Dewey Hamer a child. Closing in on seventeen daily, and growing taller at last, the young man grimaced and groaned as he struggled to match Alice's dance steps. Willie himself managed better. Ellen was a mirror to his movements, and her grace compensated for his energy. If his foot had been sound, they might have danced all night. As it was, he halted after the second waltz.

"Mrs. Trent, would you do me the honor?" Sheriff Livingston asked, stepping over and offering a hand.

"Thank you, no," Ellen answered. "Willie and I were about to sit for awhile."

"Still lame, huh?" Livingston asked. "Well, I'm at your service, ma'am. And you'll find all my limbs in perfect health."

"I'm sure," Ellen said, turning her back on the lawman. She then led Willie to a wooden bench outside the barn, and they sat together in the moonlight and watched the stars overhead. Only later, as a certain uneasiness settled over them, did Willie note the white picket fence behind them. A single stone stood within the pickets.

ALBERT, BELOVED SON was etched in the marble.

"So all's not forgotten, after all," Ellen whispered.

"Never is," Willie noted.

The real proof of that statement came minutes later when a rider raced past the barn, reined his horse to a halt, and fell into the dust-choked road, muttering a warning.

"What's he babbling about?" Thurman Livingston asked.

"Riders!" the cowboy screamed, turning so that everyone saw the bloody mess that had been his left shoulder. "Mr. Mills . . ."

Further words were unnecessary, for a column of dust rolled toward them in the faint moonlight, and pounding hooves warned of approaching trouble.

"Quick, to the wagon!" Willie yelled, urging Ellen into motion. He then limped to where the boys stood, jaws open wide, and led them to safety.

Joe Eagle had already captured Annie and carried her to the wagon. The Cheyenne had one of the rifles aimed toward the unwelcome guests even before Willie arrived with the boys.

"Who is it?" Ellen asked, as she hugged the children close to her.

"Who else?" Willie asked in turn. "Riley Rucker."

Indeed it was. But this time Rucker wasn't leading a band of cousins and neighbors. No, there were five men at his side, and Willie recognized every face from a poster that had crossed his desk while serving as Esperanza's marshal.

"Those are the Calder brothers," Willie muttered, as he took the second Winchester. The redheads flanked Rucker. The taller was Burt. Ben, the younger, had a wicked scar on his left cheek to remind him of a south Texan killed over a hand of cards near Fort Griffin.

"Alex Murphy's the one in black," Joe noted. "Me and Marshal Cobb trailed him up in Kansas. We had dealin's with George Otus there, too," Joe added, pointing to an older man bringing up the rear.

"And the young one?" Willie asked, searching his memory.

"Perry Kidd," Joe announced. "Nineteen, they say, and he's kilt eight or nine men already."

Willie remembered each poster. Except for Murphy, the outlaws had made their reputations in New Mexico Territory, hiring out on either side of one range war or another. They were just the sort to bring on such a ride—cold, heartless killers, who wouldn't flinch from anything.

"It's the Ruckers!" little Jake Mills screamed, as he dashed toward the house.

Thurm Livingston recognized them, too, and he hurried to warn his boss. He'd gotten to within five feet of Mills when the Calder brothers cut him down.

A pair of cowboys raced out of the barn, revolvers drawn, and got off a few shots before they died in a volley of bullets. One managed to put a hole through George Otus, and the raider clapped a hand to his forehead, tumbled, and died.

"Grab the boys there," Riley ordered, and the Calders trapped Jake and Jonathan against the barn. Loretta made a rush toward her children but Perry Kidd, a wicked grin on his face, ran her down. As she floundered in the dust, Kidd shot her three times.

"Perry, the girl's gettin' away!" Ben shouted, and Kidd turned his attentions to Alice.

"Hold it, honey!" Kidd warned, but Alice was already prying a pistol from George Otus's hand.

"No, Alice!" Dewey shouted from a corner of the woodpile. The girl raised the gun, though, and Kidd fired. Alice collapsed like a rag doll, a swelling red circle staining her delicate lace dress. Dewey rushed over, palms open so the grinning Perry Kidd could note he was unarmed.

"Well, she'd've likely been more trouble than amusement," Kidd explained to an angry Riley Rucker. "Them two'll do."

By now the Calders had wrestled Jake and Jonathan onto their horses and rejoined the pack.

"Aim to make a fight of it, Major?" Riley called to the wagon then.

"Is it a fight you want?" Willie answered.

"No, it's twenty-five thousand dollars," Riley explained, tossing a note toward Abner Mills. The rancher stood beside his wife's corpse, frozen in shock and dismay. "Bring it to Blood Mesa at dusk tomorrow. Elsewise, I'll return your youngsters the way you sent mine back to me!"

The Calders raced off with their captives, followed by Murphy. Rucker and Kidd waited a bit to insure against pursuit.

"Why don't you shoot them!" Mills shouted at Willie. "You've got rifles!"

"Want your boys back?" Willie asked, feeling the cold steel in his hands as he peered down at Ellen and the children. He wouldn't endanger them. Not again!

"Long as we're waitin', I'll have a look through the house," Kidd announced, dismounting. The killer trotted over to the porch and ambled along inside.

"There's just the one!" Mills screamed. "Kill him! Shoot the devil!"

"Major knows who the devil is," Riley said calmly.

162

"Knows the Calders, too. I don't come back, there'll be pieces of them boys all over this country."

Mills shuddered. Meanwhile, the crash of fine china and the sounds of upset furniture attested to Perry Kidd's ransacking of the house. The young outlaw emerged from the house waving a flour sack. As he mounted, Riley turned to face Mills.

"Remember, Mills," Riley repeated. "Twenty-five thousand in cash. Dusk tomorrow. Blood Mesa. Come alone, too, if you aim to see those boys again."

"You've already got my cash!" Mills pleaded. "On the stage, at the hotel, and at the bank. I couldn't raise that much money in a month!"

"Oh, you'll figure a way," Kidd said, grinning as he pulled a pearl necklace from the sack and draped it around his neck.

"I'd have to sell everything!" Mills shouted. "And who is there who'd buy?"

"That'd be your worry," Riley replied, glaring at the rancher with unbridled hatred. "At least you got a chance to bring those two back. More'n you give me!"

Rucker turned his horse and galloped off down the road. Kidd followed more slowly, waving a pistol and firing off shots to deter any would-be pursuers. They were gone a moment later. In all, the raiders had come and gone in half an hour.

As the dust and powder smoke cleared, Abner Mills regained his senses. Dewey had managed to plug the hole in Alice's side, and Ellen now turned her skill to the problem. As for Loretta Mills, Thurman Livingston, and the dead ranch hands, they were left to the preacher.

"Men, gather close," Mills announced, once he was assured Alice was in good hands. "You've seen what's happened. Who'll ride with me this night to bring my boys home?"

"I know them Calders," one old-timer declared. "Better

163

to pay the money, boss. Those boys ain't the kind to tangle with.''

"I'll pay well!" Mills assured them. "Hundred dollars a man, and you'll all share equal in the reward money. I understand there's better than five thousand dollars on the bunch of them, and I'll match that for Riley Rucker's hide.''

"You got the money?'' the old-timer asked.

"Let's see the cash,'' another added.

"I'll get it,'' Mills assured them.

"Excuse me, boss, but we ain't been paid last month's wages yet,'' a young hand said, shifting his weight under Mills's icy glare. "I ain't complainin', as you feed us regular, and there's little work elsewhere. But you're askin' us to ride against men who cut their teeth with bowie knives. A hundred dollars in my hand wouldn't be enough for me to get kilt over.''

The others murmured their agreement, and Mills shouted angrily.

"You all feel that way, the devil take you! I got a dead wife and a bleeding daughter to look after. If you won't ride with me, then clear out. You're all of you fired!''

"Better that than dead,'' the old-timer answered, and the others nodded their agreement.

An hour later the ranch was nearly deserted. A simple wooden cross stood beside Albert's headstone, and fifty feet away a small forest of similar crosses marked the final resting places of George Otus, Thurm Livingston, and the others. The cowboys had delayed their departure long enough to bury the dead.

Outside Mills's big house Willie paced beside the wagon. Joe sat in the bed, stroking Annie's walnut hair and whispering stories to the three anxious boys. Dewey sat on the porch steps, nervously tapping his fingers on the boards.

Eventually Ellen walked out, her face pale and her fingers numb from effort.

"Maybe Jack would have managed it,'' she told Willie.

"Me, I couldn't. She'll rest quiet a while. Likely it'll be over sometime before dawn."

She must have told Mills as much, for he emerged moments later.

"You know the country, Fletcher," the rancher declared. "And the man behind this. What's more, you have a tender heart toward youngsters. I've noticed that. There's money in it—rewards from a dozen banks and the stage line. I'll add any sum you ask."

"Why not just pay the ransom?" Ellen suggested.

"I don't have it," Mills said, dropping his chin onto his chest. "They took everything I had left, even Loretta's jewels. In time—selling my stock, the ranch—I can raise plenty. But now?"

"It wouldn't matter," Willie said, trembling as he took Ellen's hand. "It's not the money Riley wants. The others, sure, but I saw him sitting there, holding Levi. It's you he wants, Mills. Sooner or later he'll kill you."

"And the boys?" Ellen asked.

"Don't know," Willie confessed. "I'd wager them, too."

"You will bring them home, won't you?" Mills pleaded. "You can have Livingston's job. Anything."

"No, Willie!" Ellen cried.

"There's nobody else to do it," he told her.

"You'll have my undying gratitude," Mills said, clasping Willie's hands.

"Sure," Willie mumbled, as he pulled away and turned toward the waiting wagon. "I'll see to this, Mills, but I also mean to see somebody pays for Levi."

"The men who did it are dead," Mills argued.

"And the one who ordered it?" Willie asked.

The wagon was halfway back to Salt Fork Crossing when Joe Eagle spoke for everyone.

"You gone crazy, Major," the Cheyenne declared. "Who's he to ask favors?"

"I'm not doing it for him," Willie explained, as he gazed at the children sleeping in the back of the wagon. "No matter who their papa is, those boys haven't earned what Riley's got in mind. You were at Sand Creek. Has anybody ever merited being chopped to pieces?"

"I'm goin' along," Dewey announced, lifting his head and nodding somberly.

"Well, three ain't a bad number for a posse, even if they're all crazed for goin'," Joe said, laughing to himself. "Never dreamed to die for such as Mills."

"Blood Mesa, huh?" Dewey added. "Joe's always said it's a place best left be."

"Bad medicine," Joe said sourly. "Knew it first time I saw the place."

CHAPTER 19

After passing a restless night, Willie awoke even earlier than Joe the following morning. He tenderly eased Annie's head off his left arm and managed to crawl away from his blankets without rousing Billy or Cobb, who were huddled close to his right side.

Best leave them to find some rest, Willie told himself. He didn't know if there would be much later.

Ellen found him in the kitchen, stuffing a flour sack with a smoked ham and some dried beef. She added biscuits, a couple of onions, and four carrots.

"I wish you'd stay," she whispered, as she spread bacon strips on a hot griddle.

"You know I have to go," he answered. "Please, Ellie, no more arguments. And no good-byes. We've done it too many times. I'll be back."

"Will you?"

"Yes," he insisted. "I'm an old hand at this business. And I have help."

"An addle-headed Indian and a half-grown boy?"

"Dewey's a good shot, and he'll do what he's told. As to Joe, well, I couldn't ask for better. He's hunted this sort of dark-hearted men before."

"Bring him back, Willie," Ellen urged. "Annie'll have your head if anything happens to her Joe."

"Nothing will."

"I do wish you'd leave Dewey here," she said, as she turned the bacon. "Tell him I was nervous and asked him to guard the house."

"He'd see through it," Willie argued.

"He's seen enough death in his young life."

"I celebrated my seventeenth birthday burying friends in Virginia," Willie answered. "I'd been at war two years."

"I hope he never turns as hard as you, Willie Delamer."

"So do I," Willie agreed.

Dewey walked into the kitchen then, and Ellen turned her attention to breakfast. Joe arrived moments later, followed by the drowsy children. No one said much as Ellen slapped bacon and eggs onto plates. Even when the last bite had been consumed, the room remained eerily silent.

After clearing the table, Willie headed outside and began collecting equipment. Dewey saddled the horses, together with two spare mounts he hoped would be needed to carry the Mills boys home. Joe checked the rifles and loaded each Winchester with its full fifteen shells. The Cheyenne tied an extra rifle behind his saddle and stuffed boxes of shells into his saddlebags.

Willie buckled on a pair of shiny Colt pistols and slid a pocket gun into his boot. He added a knife, knowing it would either be a long-range fight or a melee at close quarters.

"If they're on Blood Mesa, we'll have an easy time of it," Joe boasted. "Lots of ways to sneak up on a man there."

"Or ambush one," Willie noted.

But Riley Rucker wasn't on Blood Mesa.

It was Joe who picked up the trail with his sharp eyes. It led past the mesa and on to Tonkawa Creek. Willie frowned as he stared at the open country ahead. From the creek a man could spot riders half a mile away.

"There they are," Joe announced, pointing to a thin wisp of smoke. "Fine place they picked, out in the open, with no cover to speak of."

Willie nodded. Only clumps of sagebrush and mounds of prickly pear broke the flat stretch of plain. Surprise was unlikely. There was a chance of catching them unawares come nightfall, but Riley wouldn't wait past dusk. No, come sundown Jake and Jonathan Mills would be dead.

"Best we hide the horses here," Joe suggested, pointing to a line of willows at the base of a hill. "I'll have a look at the camp."

Willie nodded, and Joe dismounted. The Cheyenne left behind his rifles and went ahead alone. Willie helped Dewey secure the horses out of view. Then there was nothing to do but wait for Joe's return.

Joe crept stealthily along the sandy ground, using the scant cover to conceal his slithering body. His buckskins blended into the sandy soil, and he was virtually invisible. Nevertheless, Willie was relieved when Joe returned to the cover of the willows.

"Won't be easy," the Cheyenne declared, dropping to one knee and smoothing out a square of sand with his right hand. Joe then traced the camp with his finger. On one side of the creek Alex Murphy stood guard over the horses. On the far bank the Calders lounged around a fire, jabbering away like a pair of magpies. Riley Rucker was with them, but he seemed distracted.

"And Kidd?" Willie asked.

"I didn't see him," Joe said, frowning. "Might've been inside the tent."

"What tent?" Dewey asked.

"Here," Joe said, marking an X behind the fire. "That's sure to be where they've got the boys."

"Five men, and one out of view," Willie said, considering the problem.

"I can get to Murphy easy," Joe boasted. "The horses, too. I get him and the horses, they might leave the boys unguarded."

"Scant chance of that," Willie declared. "Any way to circle around, come in from the back side?"

"Not even a shadow to cover you there," Joe explained. "Camp's on a slope, and they'd see you comin'."

"So we have to cross the creek," Willie said, frowning. "Poor odds."

"We have to try," Dewey argued.

"Good way to get shot," Joe declared. "How you want to do it, Major?"

"Joe, take Dewey along with you this time. Crawl up on Murphy as you planned, only leave Dewey so he can watch the camp. Dewey, your job's to keep the ones at the fire away from that tent."

"And you?" Dewey asked, gazing nervously at Willie.

"Perry Kidd's my job," Willie told them, "in the tent or out. He'll stop us otherwise."

"Use the creek, Major," Joe suggested. "A careful man can make his way along the bank without the ones at the fire seein' him."

"Murphy would," Dewey warned.

"Murphy'll be dead," Joe said, grimly drawing the knife from his boot. "Ready?"

"No, but it won't get easier," Willie told them. "Best we get to it."

Joe nodded, then led Dewey from the trees. The two of them crept cautiously from one clump of sagebrush to the next, their bellies on the ground, fearful of making any stray movement. They raised no dust and made no sound. Finally, with Dewey in position twenty feet from the campfire, Joe continued toward Alex Murphy.

That was Willie's cue. He now started along the bank, doing his best to stay within the shadows. It wasn't easy, for the midday sun was standing high in a cloudless sky.

Maybe if Alex Murphy had remained with the horses, Joe

would have caught him unawares. It might then have been possible for Willie to reach the tent unseen. But all plans have the bad habit of coming apart, and that's exactly what happened.

First, Alex Murphy, growing restless, walked down to the creek and called to his companions.

"You promised me coffee, remember!" Murphy shouted.

"Take him a cup," Riley said, motioning to Ben Calder.

"I ain't nobody's fetch-boy," Ben grumbled. "Let him come get it."

"He's watchin' the horses," Burt pointed out.

"Well I'm watchin' this fire!" Ben growled.

"Fools," Perry Kidd said, marching out of the tent and filling a cup from a pot of steaming liquid. Kidd then continued to the shallow creek. Halfway there he spotted Joe Eagle.

"Behind you, Murphy!" Kidd shouted, as he tossed the cup aside and pulled his pistol.

Joe rolled clear of Kidd's well-aimed fire, but the plan was ruined. Willie did manage to dig himself a hole along the bank and send Kidd scurrying back to the fire. But the Calders and Riley Rucker soon added their guns to the fight and bullets spattered the rocky ground, forcing Willie back.

"Mills?" Riley called, once it was clear the attack had failed.

"No, Riley, it's me!" Willie hollered.

"Well, Major, it's sure a surprise you're here!" Riley said, signaling his companions to cease firing. "Ole Mills wouldn't come himself, eh?"

"He's tending his daughter," Willie explained.

"No, he's just got no stomach for a fair fight," Riley said angrily. "So, what's it to be?"

"I've come to fetch those boys along home," Willie explained. "Same as I tried to bring Levi back to you."

"Them boys ain't goin' nowhere till we get the money!" Kidd shouted.

"There's no money left," Willie replied. "You took it all."

"Oh, there's money, all right," Kidd argued. "Should've seen the inside o' that fellow's house!"

"Money's not the point," Riley added. "You know that, Willie."

"Haven't you had enough revenge?" Willie yelled.

"Not nearly."

"Mrs. Mills is dead," Willie said, frowning. "The girl likely didn't last through the night. How about some compassion, Riley? Those boys never hurt you. Killing 'em won't give you any satisfaction."

"Oh, I don't know," Riley argued. "You never been a father, Willie. Never felt the hurt of losin' a boy. I lost two now. Sooner or later Mills'll think things over. Then he'll come for his boys."

"No, I'll be bringing 'em back myself," Willie declared.

"You come on, mister, and you'll take a couple o' corpses back!" Ben Calder vowed.

"You move toward that tent, Riley, I'll pepper your hide," Willie warned.

"Don't have to," Riley explained. "I got a shotgun here that'll blow that tent and them boys both plum to hell. Think that over, won't you?"

"Riley, don't!" Willie pleaded. "Remember . . ."

"Remember what?" Riley shouted. "Virginia? I remember Levi dyin' in my arms. Poor boy was cut to pieces! I got no more memory for anything else!"

Willie sighed. There was nothing left to do. He stared at the tent, at the killers lurking behind the fire, and realized there was no chance of a rescue. Reluctantly he retreated back along the creek, trying not to imagine the frightened boys inside that tent.

Joe crawled back to the willows, too, leaving Dewey to watch the camp from cover.

CHAPTER 20

In time Dewey, too, retreated to the willows. There he sat and waited for Willie to come up with a second plan.

"Ain't nothin' we can do," Joe finally announced, as Willie opened the provision sack and passed out food. "Ride down on 'em, but they'd likely kill us."

"And the boys for certain," Willie muttered. "It was a close thing, Joe. Almost had 'em."

"There's time yet," Joe declared, as he turned a biscuit over in his hands.

"They won't do anything till dusk," Willie said, studying the creek and the camp beyond. "Come afternoon, the sun'll hang low in the west. If we circle around and come in that way, the sun'll be in their eyes."

"No cover at all out that way," Joe argued. "It'd be a chance, though."

"Best chance," Willie declared. "Dewey, you still have your shooter's eye?"

"I'd better," the boy said, gazing grimly at the creek.

"There's no other way to bring those boys out alive," Willie told his friends. "And that's what I plan to do."

*　　*　　*

And so they waited, as the sun crept slowly across the sky. From time to time the camp would stir. Sometimes Perry Kidd would walk out and holler toward the willows. Mostly the outlaws kept to their camp, though.

As the sun hung low in the western sky, Blood Mesa took on first an amber and later a scarlet tint. A buzzard turned slow circles over the creek, lending its ominous presence to the scene.

"That old man come yet, Major?" Riley Rucker shouted from the far side of the creek.

"He bring the money?" Kidd added.

Their words were directed at the willows, though, and Willie wasn't there. For better than an hour he, Joe Eagle, and Dewey Hamer had been circling the camp, crawling up the rocky slope of the mesa and moving in on the outlaw camp from behind.

It was an old trick, using the sun to mask an approach. Willie recalled a dozen tales of similar tactics, learned while he was riding with old Yellow Shirt's band back in the late fifties. If you judged a body by his size, Willie was a boy back then. But he remembered everything, and as he crawled ever closer he used every ounce of memory and experience to advantage.

"Cut their horses off, Joe," Willie said, as they approached along the creek. "Stay close," he told Dewey.

Willie could smell the campfire smoke now as it spiraled skyward. Riley and the Calder brothers remained at the fire as before. Kidd was busy filling his canteen at the creek. Alex Murphy paced back and forth on the opposite bank.

All in the open, Willie noted. But so were the boys. Jake sat only inches from scar-faced Ben Calder, and little Jonathan stirred a kettle a foot closer to the fire.

"I see somethin'!" Murphy shouted, shouldering his rifle.

Willie saw it, too, a flash as sunlight reflected off Joe's Winchester.

"It's them!" Kidd shouted, grinning at the thought of the ransom. "Mills!"

"Wrong man," Willie muttered, as he raised his own rifle and fired. Joe must have done so, too, for a pair of bullets struck Murphy simultaneously. The first lifted him off the ground, and the second slammed him down hard.

"Murph?" Kidd called, as he scrambled behind the cover of the tent.

"He's dead!" Joe shouted as he splashed through the creek and gained the safety of the horses just beyond. "You'll be, too, soon enough."

"Ain't you forgettin' somethin'?" Ben Calder shouted, dragging Jake along like a shield. The scrawny eleven-year-old didn't provide much cover, but Willie held his fire just the same.

"Toss the money over!" Burt added.

The elder Calder grabbed his rifle and crept cautiously toward the creek. Dewey shot him in the throat.

"Ben?" Burt yelled, as he stumbled. Dewey's second shot pierced both lungs, and Burt fell face-first into the muddy water.

Willie moved forward rapidly. Just ahead, Ben wrestled with Jake while trying to pull a knife.

"Kick him, Jake!" Jonathan yelled, and the older boy did just that. Ben howled, and he released his grip long enough for Jake to stumble away.

"Ben, behind you!" Kidd shouted, but Ben didn't turn in time to see Willie swing his Winchester. The barrel slammed against Ben's forehead, shattering bone and sending splinters into the young outlaw's brain. Ben Calder collapsed in agony.

Perry Kidd leaped forward and grabbed the Mills boys. His oversized left fist gripped both youngsters' arms and dragged them along, as his right hand waved a deadly Colt revolver.

"Where's the money, Mills?" Kidd screamed.

"Ain't them," Riley said, waving Kidd behind the tent.

"Well, that's their bad luck," Kidd declared, slinging

175

Jonathan hard against the ground. He then held the pistol to Jake's head and laughed.

"No!" Riley argued.

"I ain't draggin' them boys along no further, Rucker. If their pa ain't payin' for 'em, then we'll finish 'em here and now."

"He'll pay!" Riley argued.

"Ain't waitin' for Christmas, not with that gray hat and his Indian out there."

"Then leave the boys to me!" Riley insisted.

"No, you'd likely let 'em go," Kidd said, laughing. "You got to understand the way it works. These two get away, who'd pay next time? It's a matter o' principle. Besides, been four friends of mine killed doin' your biddin'. These bitty boys got to pay for that."

"No!" Riley shouted, as he raised his pistol and fired. Kidd stepped back, his face full of surprise as he turned his Colt and emptied it into Riley Rucker. The former Confederate dropped to his knees, coughed once, and died.

"Help, Pa!" Jake screamed, as Kidd turned back toward the boy and squeezed the trigger once, twice, three times. The hammer clicked as it struck empty chambers, and Kidd discarded the pistol. Laughing as blood ran down a shattered left arm, Kidd fought to dig a second Colt from its holster.

"That's the end of it," Willie declared, as he fired a single round through Kidd's forehead. The outlaw's knees buckled, and he fell backward in a heap.

"Jonathan!" Jake cried, as he fought to rouse his brother. The eight-year-old moaned and fought to catch his breath, but he wasn't hurt badly.

Willie assured himself the Calders and Kidd were dead before kneeling beside Riley Rucker.

"Why'd he do it?" Jake asked, as he helped Jonathan sit up.

"Wanted to punish your papa," Willie explained, as he

closed his old comrade's eyelids. "Had two boys of his own killed, you see."

"I know that," Jake said, staring in dismay at the bloody camp. "Why'd he save us?"

"That's harder," Willie said, gazing at the fiery sun as it died behind the mesa. "Maybe he was recalling Levi. Maybe knowing the hurt it would bring softened him."

"Maybe he was just tired of the killin'," Dewey suggested, as he stumbled to the fire.

"He was a good man once," Willie explained. "Before the world turned upside down, and everything was twisted around so he didn't know what to do anymore."

"You blaming Pa for that?" Jake asked.

"No, just saying it happened," Willie muttered. "Joe, we best collect those fellows. Be some reward dollars coming."

"I'll fetch their horses," Dewey said, turning toward the creek. "You want to bring all of 'em?"

"I'll be taking Riley to Salt Fork Crossing," Willie answered. "I don't suppose he'd mind resting down there with Warren."

"Dewey and I'll see to it," Joe said, kicking sand over the embers of the campfire. "Why don't you take them boys along home."

"Pa'd pay you," Jake said, pulling his brother close.

"You haven't learned much today, have you?" Willie asked. "There's some things you can't buy, son. No matter how much money you've got."

It was long past sundown when Willie delivered the Mills boys to their father. Both sadly noted the two fresh crosses in the graveyard and waited for an explanation.

"I owe you, Fletcher," Mills said, as he hugged the boys to his side. "Anything. Everything. The sheriff's badge is yours. And a reward. Ten thousand? Another five if you bring Rucker in."

"Haven't you paid a high enough price for revenge?" Willie asked angrily.

"Pa, Rucker's dead," Jake explained. "He died saving us."

Jonathan nodded and Mills just stood there, stunned.

"I don't believe it possible," Mills finally mumbled. "Why?"

"I guess maybe in the end he found out there was more father in him than killer," Willie suggested.

"The reward stands," Mills announced.

"Figure that will help them rest easier?" Willie asked, motioning to the graveyard. "I don't want your money, and I don't want your badge, Mills. You really want to do something?"

"Anything," Mills promised.

"Go with me to the judge in Throckmorton and tell him how you shot Polk and those fellows at the Salt Fork. Tell him about hanging Warren. About Levi."

Willie choked with emotion as he remembered it all.

"Anything else!" Mills pleaded.

"Pa, what's he talking about?" Jake asked.

"Go to the judge with me," Willie said.

"You know that's impossible," Mills said, stiffening. "And I think maybe it's time you left."

"Oh, I'm going," Willie growled. "Can't get clear of this place fast enough. If I was you I wouldn't stay too long, either. Too many know the truth. And with or without you, I aim to see that judge."

"I have friends in Austin, Fletcher. Your threats mean nothing."

"I've got friends myself," Willie warned, narrowing his eyes so that they turned the rancher cold. "And I know the truth. It's a dangerous combination, isn't it?"

Willie wasted no more words on Abner Mills. He did manage to return Jake's nervous wave and nod to little Jonathan. Then he galloped away from the Mills place and headed home.

EPILOGUE

Willie sat beside the river and watched the sun climb into the eastern sky. It promised to be a lovely morning. A spring warmth kissed the land, and the breeze was warm and gentle.

Off to his left Joe Eagle had the boys busy adding a gate to the horse corral. Ellen sat on the porch, tying a pink ribbon in Annie's hair.

The sound of a galloping horse drew their attention. All heads turned to the road, where Dewey Hamer emerged from a dust swirl, smiling out his greetings.

"Heard the news, Major?" Dewey asked as he dismounted. "Ole Abner Mills has cleared out. Sold everything and took a stagecoach south. Word is he's bound for Bolivia or some such place."

"Where'd you hear that?" Willie asked.

"In Throckmorton," Dewey explained. "I been there the last three days, remember?"

"Didn't notice," Willie lied. "I don't suppose Mills' leaving had anything to do with Judge Wells."

"The judge figured it might have," Dewey admitted. "Wondered why, though. He said we didn't have the evidence to make the charges stick."

"Mills knew who was guilty," Willie declared. "And so did everyone else, proof or no proof."

"You could be right," Dewey said, scratching his chin. "They say there'll be a lot of new folks movin' in before long. Even been talk o' rebuildin' the town. Likely call it somethin' else, though. 'Esperanza' 's deemed bad luck."

"You hear all that in Throckmorton?" Willie asked.

"And elsewhere," Dewey said, grinning.

"I've thought about moving on myself lately," Willie said, gazing at Ellen.

"Going to Kansas, Uncle Wil?" Billy called from the corral.

"Maybe," Willie replied. "Or down to the Clear Fork."

"Why?" Ellen asked, finishing Annie's bow and hurrying down to the river.

"There's too much blood on this land, Ellie," he told her.

"Well, I'll admit it holds its share of ghosts. The Clear Fork, you say?"

"This place here would make a fair horse ranch, too, of course. Joe and Dewey might consider taking it on."

"I imagine they plan on following you south."

"No, we talked on it. They figure things might be a little crowded down there, what with you and the kids."

"So we'd be going, too? Nice of you to ask me."

"Well, a man ought to ask a gal some things, I suspect. Especially if he figures maybe she ought to take his name."

"Marry?" she asked soberly.

"You said it yourself, Ellie. It's been a lot of years. Lot of hard times and bitter memories. But it's what I want more'n anything."

"Me, too."

"Best you talk to the little ones about it?"

"You're not that blind," she scolded. "They took you to heart ages ago."

"Now there's the other thing."

"Yes?"

"I've done some hard thinking about all this, and I decided if I was to ask you to take my name, it ought to be a good one."

"And?"

"I've worn a lot of handles since the war, Ellie, and I've had bum luck with all of 'em. When all's said and done, though, I'm a Delamer. That's not a name everyone in your family admires. And it's not one everyone in mine's ever been eager to share."

"You mean your brother Sam. My family's never included you in any grudge."

"We won't be far from Palo Pinto down on the Clear Fork. Sooner or later we're apt to lock horns."

"It should have happened back in '66," she argued. "We've had all these wasted years because you shied away then."

"They've not been a waste," Willie said, pointing to the youngsters. "You've done well enough."

"Maybe we'll do better."

"I plan to," he said, pulling her close.

And so on the fifth day of April, 1880, Willie Delamer and Ellen Cobb Trent exchanged vows on the banks of the Brazos River. It was as they'd always imagined it, with wildflowers crowning the hills and the bluest sky in memory promising a bright future. Travis Cobb served as best man, and among the guests were a grinning state senator named James Delamer, a young horse-breeder named Hamer, and a grinning Indian tracker everyone knew as Annie's Uncle Joe.

Friends and family ate and drank to their heart's content, for the toasts were many and the tears considerable.

"To better days," Willie said, raising his glass as the party prepared to disperse.

"Can't be a better one than this," young Billy remarked, and Willie grinned.

"To family, then," Willie suggested.

"To old friends," Ellen added.

"To happiness!" James Delamer shouted. "And to peace."

"Amen!" the crowd exclaimed.

ABOUT THE AUTHOR

G. Clifton Wisler comes by his interest in the West naturally. Born in Oklahoma and raised in Texas, he discovered early on a fascination for the history of the region. His first novel, MY BROTHER, THE WIND, received a nomination for the American Book Award in 1980. Among the many others that have followed are THUNDER ON THE TENNESSEE, winner of the Western Writers of America Spur Award for Best Western Juvenile Book of 1983; WINTER OF THE WOLF, a Spur finalist in 1982; and Delamer Westerns THE TRIDENT BRAND, STARR'S SHOWDOWN, PURGATORY, ABREGO CANYON, THE WAYWARD TRAIL, SWEETWATER FLATS, SAM DELAMER, CLEAR FORK, and NORTH OF ESPERANZA. AMONG THE EAGLES, a Delamer Western, was honored by the Western Writers as best original paperback of 1989. In addition to his writing, Wisler frequently speaks to school groups and conducts writing clinics. He lives in Plano, Texas, where he is active in Boy Scouts.